# MABEL
# HARTLEY
## and the Egyptian Vault

*Titles available in the Mabel Hartley series*
*(in reading order):*

# MABEL
# HARTLEY
## and the Egyptian Vault

J.E. Reddington

First Published in Canada in 2016 by J.E. Reddington
Copyright © J.E. Reddington 2016

www.janereddington.com

Previously published in 2014 in electronic format.
ISBN 978-1-77507-00-09 (paperback)

For my Dad, Graham.

With thanks to Gray Sutherland.

# The Egyptian Vault

# Chapter One

Everything changed over Sunday breakfast. "Mabel," my dad said, "keep your eyes open for me, would you? Your new school's come up in a case I'm working on, something to do with stolen paintings. But please stay out of trouble. Do you understand?"

"Of course I do," I said, hardly believing he'd finally handed me the keys to the kingdom – the details of a case. Before, when I'd asked him about his work, he'd always come up with some excuse to put me off. Without actually saying so, he'd insinuate that a young girl like me couldn't possibly be mature enough to be a confidante on police matters. Suddenly that had all changed and I had to pinch myself.

"We'll be driving you in, in the morning." My mum gave my dad a stern look after his referring to the paintings. She didn't want me involved in police work either. The page on the calendar said October 15, 1980. Just so you're up to speed, I'm fourteen and going into the fourth form at Hollingsworth School for Boys and Girls at Milford-on-Sea, a village down in southern England.

I have to admit I'm scared. I don't like the idea of being a new girl at the beginning of term, but it's even worse because I'm transferring from another school and starting six weeks later than everyone else. That means I'll stick out like a sore thumb and I'll get all those awful stares, which will make me want to disappear.

# The Egyptian Vault

After breakfast, Dad went back in his *strictly off limits* office. Then I had a chance to ask Mum about what Dad had said.

"Did he know about the stolen paintings before we came? Is that why he wanted me to go to Hollingsworth?"

"No, no, from what I hear the case has been passed on to every police commissioner who's ever come here. They keep hoping someone will solve it, and now there's a new element; I'm surprised he told you about it, Mabel."

"Me too. What's the new part?"

"Something to do with a gallery, but I don't know more than that, love." The gallery must have been part of the New Forest District, and in all likelihood it was operating right here in Lymington, the town we'd moved to. Lymington is about two-and-a-half hours southwest of London by train, a fiddly little place, pretty as a postcard, with narrow cobbled streets and funny little houses like ours.

My mum, Violet, is part of the cabin crew at British Airways, and that's why my parents sent me to boarding school. They think I need constant supervision, which is infuriating because I am very responsible most of the time. Last year in London, they asked me to apply for a scholarship so I could get into this school. I never thought I'd have a chance. Well, maybe I did but it was only a slim chance.

When we got the news, Dad wouldn't stop going on about how proud he felt, and rang everyone we knew to tell them. Even though I'd won the scholarship, I didn't want to go. I was already struggling with loneliness, and now I felt even more alone because I'd only be home on weekends. It made my brain hurt to think about it. But I couldn't tell my parents that. They simply wouldn't understand.

You see, even though I'm fairly grown up I still feel there's so much I can't do. Like riding a motorbike. Gosh, I can't wait to get on one of those. I like going very fast and feeling as if danger's just a breath away. I'd love a leather suit and biker boots, but Dad would have a fit if I even mentioned something like that. What I need is to meet someone who has brothers who like racing, and then I can hop on the back and ride away from everything that's holding me down.

Lymington is fairly dull, but it's a pretty little town. We live at Bosun's Locker, on Captain's Row, in a two-floor flat with an attic. I live in the room on the top floor, which Mum says she thought I'd like because it has a trap door to the roof space, so I can go out at night and see the lights on the water and get a breath of fresh air.

In the morning, I flung myself out of bed, but didn't get much further than washing my face, before the dread began to set in. You see, my hair looks terrible. Every girl's nightmare because it's so curly and sticks up in every direction. That's probably the reason no one's *ever* tried to kiss me. I would *really* like to know more about boys, but my Dad's made them off limits too. And the other thing you should know is that I stopped growing about four years ago.

I still have to stand on a stool to look at the mirror and everyone looks down on me. It's hardly fair, being so small and so desperate to make a good impression on someone. In the mirror, I wet my hair down, but it sprang back up into the usual froth of curls. I combed and combed, but to no avail. In the end I put a hat on. My favourite is a lorry driver's cap that has a Union Jack badge sewn on the back. When I'm wearing it I feel fearless - like the person I *want* to be when I grow up. I put on my new school uniform, with the grey blazer, blue kilt, black tie, pink shirt, black socks and sturdy walking shoes. Boring, but required.

Within minutes, Mum and Dad said I should come down the stairs, before I made us all late. I ran out of the door and ate my breakfast in the car. Mum had made me an egg sandwich with Marmite between the slices of bread, which usually I love but today I knew I'd smell like an egg. Yuck!

It only took a quarter of an hour to reach the school. To get up to the gates, we went down a lane with a huge column of trees on either side that spread over the car like a canopy. I would have liked it more if we'd been driving a carriage with a horse trotting ahead of us. The mud was high and when we came up over the hill the school rose up before us.

I looked at the first page of the brochure, which said,

*Hollingsworth Preparatory School was built in the 1800s, by a baron from France, but takes its name from its second owner, an Egyptologist called Edmond Hollingsworth who moved here in 1900. It has three main towers, and one bell tower. There are six smaller towers. An inner courtyard provides the school with stables for students who wish to keep their horses with them at the school.*

# The Egyptian Vault

We stopped in front of the footbridge, and I felt my heart sink because I knew I couldn't escape. The great doors opened and a boy and a girl, who looked about my age, came out. I took a deep breath and crossed my fingers, hoping they'd be nice and not snobs.

The girl's red hair skimmed her shoulders. She looked a bit chubby and her socks slouched down her legs. She kept pulling at the edge of her jumper. But when she saw me, she waved and I felt better.

The boy waved too, and I felt butterflies in my tummy. He smiled and pushed the blond curly hair out of his eyes. I wanted to faint on the spot. The closer I got, the more I wished my parents would completely disappear. We hadn't even got out of the car yet, and I felt embarrassed being with them.

"Right then Mabel, this is it I suppose," Dad said. I could see he had tears in his eyes, and I felt guilty. He's always been the emotional one, something I didn't inherit from him, but I knew that we couldn't all be weepy or we'd never get out of the car.

"Thanks for coming with me. It looks like I'm in good hands now."

"It does, doesn't it?" Dad didn't move.

"Shall we?" Mum said. "We'd best let her be on her way."

Mum got out first, and Dad followed her to the back of the car to unload my bags. I let them give me a bit of a hug before I stepped back.

"Looks like you've got ready-made friends here." Mum looked as if she didn't want to leave.

# The Egyptian Vault

"We've been waiting for you. If you're Mabel Hartley, that is," the boy said.

"I promise we won't bite, will we Hugh? I'm Tabitha Mason." She reached out her hand. I shook it. "But you can call me Tabby. I'm going to be your shadow. This is Hugh McGinley, and he's the helper from the boys' side, the best one of the lot."

"Bye then," I said to Mum and Dad. Dad wiped his cheek, and a moment or two later they got into the car and drove away.

Before I knew it, Tabby had linked arms with me.

"Hollingsworth can be a bit intimidating," Hugh said, "but I'm sure you found that out during your interview?"

"Actually I didn't have an interview, I'm here on scholarship. I wrote the exams at my old school."

They stared at each other for a little too long.

"Well full marks for you, Mabel," Tabby said. "Is that even your real name?"

"Of course it is," Hugh said. "She wouldn't call herself that if she didn't have to, would you?"

Nobody liked my name, including me; only Dad liked it because he'd known someone with that name who meant lot to him. I can't tell you how many times I've tried to get him to tell me about the other Mabel and why he thought his daughter ought to be named after her. All he'd only say was that the other Mabel had done something heroic. Mum even encouraged me to live up to my namesake.

I wanted to know more about the other Mabel. What had she done? How had they known her? Could I meet her? Neither of them would even give me a hint about her. After a while I stopped asking but I never stopped wondering.

6

# The Egyptian Vault

Tabby and Hugh realized I didn't want to talk about my name because I'd gone all quiet. Walking up the stairs, I could see the back of my parents' car now, and I wished they'd come back and fetch me.

Hugh picked up my bag, and that in itself made me feel like staying. He looked at me.

"You might want to take your hat off, Mabel, however nice it looks; the staff probably won't think much of it if you don't."

When I took it off he looked at me. "That's better," he said and I felt another storm of butterflies.

First, they took me up through the Great Hall, with all its wood paneling, a fine mantelpiece and fireplace on one side and a bench on the other, probably for people being called into the headmaster, Mr. Pearson's, office.

At the far end of the hall was an intricately carved wall made out of wood, with two doors: one for going in and the other for coming out.

"That's called an ornamental screen," Tabby said as we passed through the door below. "Once we're through on the other side, we'll go up the stairs to the dormitory. We're going to be in the same room, you know. I'm chuffed about that. No one's won the Wilton Scholarship for years so you must be incredibly clever."

I didn't know what to say and it didn't seem to matter.

"I'm quite clever too. I have a photographic memory, and that's why they asked me to lead tours of the school over the summer. It's easy to talk to strangers once you get the hang of it. My parents are horrified because I want to be an actress. Do you like being on stage, Mabel?"

"Can't stand it. Not my thing at all."

Hugh laughed and nodded and I couldn't be sure what he was thinking. Next we came into another great hall with three large archways that Tabby said had been brought from Turkey by Edmond Hollingsworth himself. I saw three columns, and a lovely wide staircase full to the brim with students on their way down to where we were.

I wanted to stop in front of the white marble busts mounted on pedestals but there didn't seem to be time. As we got up to the landing, before the staircase turned again, Tabby told us to look at the jaguars on the newel posts. They clutched shields embossed with the school crest.

Tabby looked at the shield. "See the fist in the middle? It's holding arrows, and I can tell you, there are more than a few girls around here that I'd like to use those arrows on."

When we got close to the top of the staircase, I heard a voice above us.

"Look what the cat's dragged in. Another stray."

"Speak of the devil herself," Tabby whispered to me.

"So this must be the latest charity case. And what are you called?" She stared intently at me.

"Mabel Hartley," I looked her right in the eye feeling the hair on the back of my neck stand up.

"I see." I noticed her long cat-like body and thought she and Hugh would make a handsome couple. My dad would have called her a galloping hairgrip. I smiled thinking of it.

"That's Edwina Corrigan," Tabby whispered to me.

"You wouldn't happen to be related to a Bernard Hartley, a snivelling little police officer would you? How they let these common types in, I'll never know." She raised her head and looked out over the sea of students, as if she was holding court.

"Yes, he's my father, and he's chief inspector of the New Forest District."

"You charity cases don't belong here, or anywhere else for that matter. Mind you stay out of my way and tell your father to do the same."

"Mabel can go where she likes," Tabby said. "And I'll be right behind her."

"As head girl, I'm not obliged to speak to your kind. Fatness doesn't become anyone, Tabitha, especially porky redheads."

"Edwina, stop it," Hugh said.

She smiled at the lap-dog girls beside her. "Hugh, I'm always available if you're ready to stop doing community service," she purred. Then she pushed past Tabitha, and with a sneer she was gone.

"The only saving grace is that she's in the fifth form, so we won't have all our classes with her," Tabby said. "But don't take it to heart; as you can see she's mean to the core. Must be all that family inbreeding. Her family has piles of money. Her father even owns a gallery."

Now at the top of the staircase, I looked ahead and could see another room that took my breath away.

"This is the Cartoon Gallery," Tabby said. "These seven large tapestries were designed by

The Egyptian Vault

Raphael Cartoons, a High Renaissance painter in 1515. They came from Hampton Court before they went off to the Victoria and Albert Museum in London. These are replicas, of course. That part's not in the brochure. Often I add some of my own material to mix it up a bit. People seem to like that."

I looked at Hugh, who rolled his eyes. At the end of the hall, a white marble fireplace had been carved ornately from the mantel up to the ceiling. All along the walls portraits and paintings of Renaissance life made the room feel regal. Chests and a mirror with a gilded frame made me feel as if I'd moved to a museum. I couldn't believe I'd be living here.

"Here we are." Tabby guided me over to the first door on the left. "Look: there's our names." She pointed to a list on the door, and on it I saw my name under Tabby's, along with six others.

We went in, and the room had the same white carved ceiling and eight single beds, each with its own bedside table. Our beds were next to the door, each with a pink eiderdown and a white pillowcase. I wondered about the other girls. I hoped they'd be as easy as Tabby but I knew I ought to prepare myself for the worst. Some of them might even be friends of Edwina's.

"All the girls sleep on this floor and the boys' dormitories are three floors up," Tabby said.

"We'd best get down to chapel." Hugh put my suitcase on my bed.

"We'll skip it today as this is Mabel's first day."

"So nice to meet you, Mabel," Hugh said. He looked as if he wanted to shake my hand, but we just stared at each other awkwardly for a few moments. "I'm really looking forward to showing you about." I didn't want him to go but there seemed no reason for him to stay either.

When he'd gone, Tabby said, "Finally, I've got you to myself. Now come quickly, we've got to get you to period one. It's a shame, because we shan't have time to drop these books off at the library."

"But can't we do that later?" I asked.

"Yes, the library's not going anywhere. I wanted to show you something, that's all, but it will have to wait for now."

"What is it?"

"A diary that's been locked up as long as I've been here and seeing that you're a detective's daughter you *might* be just the person to help me get at it."

"Tabby, you wouldn't know anything about some stolen paintings would you?"

"Where?"

"Here, at the school. My dad mentioned something about them. I'd like to try and find them."

"The diary might be the best place to start; are you up for taking a look?"

"I thought you'd never ask." I knew she was just the sort of girl I'd been waiting to meet my whole life.

# Chapter Two

After the first day I started to feel better about being at Hollingsworth. In the morning, we have breakfast from 7.15 to 7.45. Then tutor and registration from 8.30 to 8.40, and the others have chapel from 8.40 to 9.00. I don't have to go to chapel, because my parents can't make up their minds what they want to be, so Tabby told everyone that my family had converted to Buddhism.

Our first class is in the most fantastic room, with great arches supporting the ceiling that span the width of the room. There are benches on either side that go down the length of the room. In front of each row of benches is a table where we take our notes.

When I came through the door, I saw Hugh, with a seat he'd saved for me from our last class, and then ghastly Edwina behind us. Mr. Reeves, the art history teacher, had a small but very pointy mouth and an eyeglass in his left eye.

"Now today," he began, coming to the centre of the room, "I'd like to start by welcoming Mabel Hartley to the class. Mabel has won the Wilton Scholarship, so we'll be expecting great things from her. I hear you're from London, Mabel?"

"Yes."

"Let's start by exploring your knowledge of the history of art, particularly the Impressionists. You'll have to get used to me putting you on the spot, Mabel, but I feel sure you can impart some knowledge to us, being from London and all."

# The Egyptian Vault

I wanted to tell him that my family came from Wales, not London, but Dad's job meant we moved about every few years. I certainly didn't feel like a Londoner. I'd had a chance to explore some of the galleries there with Mum on her time off. Mum liked the Victoria and Albert Museum best, but I always wanted to go back to the Tate Gallery.

Clearing my throat, I said, "I think they experimented with colour. Monet made the water lilies famous, and Van Gogh's trademark sunflowers always stand out." I could hear how vapid it sounded and again I felt embarrassed.

"Is that all?" Mr. Reeves sighed.

I nodded but I wanted to tell him that given a chance, I could brush up on things and come up with much more.

"Very impressive, Mabel. No wonder you won the scholarship."

"Dazzling really, your comprehension of art," Edwina hissed behind me, then gave the back of my arm a hard pinch that felt like a needle in my arm.

"If I could expand a little on what you've said, Mabel, the Impressionists painted true colour and light, but Van Gogh belonged to the Expressionistic group that emerged in the late 19th century. These two groups will be the focus of our tour of the Tate Gallery in November."

"Edwina just pinched me. Has she ever done that to you?" I asked Tabby.

"She's beastly to everyone, Mabel, but I'm sure we'll think of a way to sort her out. We just need a little time."

"Sort who out?" Hugh leaned over.

"Edwina."

Mr. Reeves, picked up a riding whip from his desk and snapped it on the corner of our table. "Because of your lacklustre performance, Mabel, I feel you need another chance to impress us. Take the next week to prepare a summary of the Expressionists for us. That will be all."

+++

"You mustn't worry about her, you know," Tabby said.

"Who?" We lined up to be let into the dining room for supper.

"Edwina. You are far superior to her in every way. The fact is she's jealous of you. And besides, if we stick with Hugh, we'll be fine because she dotes on Hugh, wants him for herself really. She won't do anything spiteful if he's with us."

After Mr. Reeve's History of Art class, we went on to periods two and three, English and Science. After lunch Hugh and Tabby decided to take me on a real tour of the rest of the school grounds. The estate had been converted into a school with volleyball and tennis courts and a large sports hall. There was a gymnasium with very shiny floors and a weight training room beside it. I felt dwarfed by the splendour of it all.

Outside, we saw the football and hockey fields and further on, a spinney, like a wooded play area, with a lovely oak tree that Tabby called Mr. Trickles. Then we walked on to the lake, which the school used for rowing and sailing regattas.

"You know, when I came here," Tabby said, "I didn't want to be away from home, but now I can't

# The Egyptian Vault

imagine it any other way. You do get used to it, don't you, Hugh?"

"Yes, it's better than being at home, but then I'd take just about anywhere over home," he said.

"Why's that?" I asked.

"It's complicated and depressing. My mum's a bit of a nutter, and that's all to do with my dad. But I don't feel much like talking about that now."

"Let's go to the library," Tabby said.

Once we reached the footbridge and went through the front hall, we walked to another great room. When we were almost at the end Hugh pulled open the door for us.

"After you, Mabel."

The library had two floors, a main floor and an upper floor, both covered in walnut-panelling with a carved, black-marble fireplace. Wall-to-wall bookshelves, two stories high, made the room feel about a mile long. It also had lots of antiques and art as decoration, such as the ancient side chairs that looked as if they ought to be covered in plastic.

"Those are Ming Dynasty urns," Tabby said. "The walnut panelling goes all the way around the room, and if you look above the fireplace, you'll see a walnut frame with a tapestry of Romans at a table wearing their plumed helmets."

On either side of the tapestry I could see the figures of two ladies, carved out of dark wood. They looked as tall as me, and the one closest to me held a sphere that, had she been real, she might have tossed in the air.

Above the tapestry, I could see the estate's coat of arms. To the right of the fireplace I noticed a swirling, circular staircase that looked like a lift you might ride up inside. The stairs were supported on four columns.

On the second floor, more bookcases held floor-to-ceiling shelves. Above each shelf a gargoyle had been carved into the walnut-panelling. Looking up, I could see a painting on the ceiling.

"It's called The Chariots of Aurora, by Giovanni Pellegrini," Tabby said. "People on the tour can't get enough of it. Originally it came from the Pisani Palace in Venice. The mural depicts the dawn and symbolizes the light of learning."

"So why do they hold the tours?" I asked.

"To make money. Mr. Pearson came up with the idea of opening the grounds to tourists and they even have weddings here on the back lawn, but only in July and August. He thinks we should be part of the National Trust or something. He's all about promoting the estate, when really he ought to be taking the summer off."

In the corner, I noticed a lovely bench seat in the window and beside it, a glass case.

"That's where they keep the diary." Tabby took my hand. "Shall we take a look?"

I gave the top of the case a tug. "Locked, just as you said it would be." Inside I could see a leather-bound volume that looked at least 100 years old.

"I heard the diary turned up about five years ago," Hugh said.

"But they won't let anyone get anywhere near it," Tabby said.

"Why not?" I asked.

"Tabitha Mason," someone called and all three of us almost jumped out of our skins.

# The Egyptian Vault

"It's her," Hugh whispered. "Ms. Asquith, the librarian."

Looking around, we saw a set of mobile steps moving toward us. It had six steps in all and looked like a dragon's back. Ms. Asquith, a tiny bird-like creature, pushed it along from behind. She looked about thirty years old and she wore a navy skirt and blazer with tiny navy buttons down the front. On her lapel, I saw a dazzling brooch, in a fan of diamonds. I wanted to ask her about it, but before I could Tabby said, "What a lovely pin. Is that real?"

"Heavens, no. I just wear it for fun, it's costume jewellery. This must be *the* Mabel Hartley with you, Tabby. I've heard all about you, Mabel. We're so pleased you've come. How are you finding things?"

"A bit overwhelming to be quite honest. But I do like all these rooms: they feel as if they're from another world."

"That's Edmond's taste. His work took him mostly to Egypt and I suppose he wanted a little reminder of it back here in England. That's him over there." She turned to face a portrait hanging over the circulation desk.

The man in the portrait had a long white beard. He wore a black robe over his jacket and tie and had combed his thick white hair back. His hands, claw-like, clasped the armrests of his chair. On his left little finger was a tiny golden ring.

"He first published journals on the pyramids and temples of Giza," Ms. Asquith said. "He discovered the city of Naucratis and a Middle Kingdom temple with the earliest known alphabet. Some say Egypt came to be an obsession for him. I'm sure his daughter, Emily, would have agreed."

She nodded at the cabinet with the diary inside. "It's a shame the key can't be given for you to see for yourselves. I'm told her diary contains all sorts of secrets about the estate. Lovely to meet you, Mabel. Do come by again if you should ever need anything." She rolled the steps away back to the circulation desk.

"What you do know about Emily?" I asked.

"I think her father died when she was still very young," Hugh said.

"Then her uncle inherited the estate and kicked her out," Tabby said.

"Where did she go?"

"No one knows. Perhaps she wrote about what happened in the diary." Tabby looked over eagerly. "Shall we come up with a plan to get it out then?"

"Why would we want to do that?" Hugh said.

"Because it might have some information about some stolen paintings," I said.

"But what about your scholarship? If we got caught, you'd lose it and be expelled!" Hugh said.

"I know, but we shan't get caught, and I'd like to try and see if I can get it out. My dad even said I should keep my eyes open for any information about these paintings they've been trying to track down at his work, and that's what I'm doing."

"You're either in or out, Hugh," Tabby said, "but if you're out then you'll have to promise not to tell a soul what we're planning to do."

"It would be for a good reason, to help with the case," he replied. "We could just borrow the diary for a quick look and we might be able to find another book to put inside the case and they'd never know the difference. I'm sure I could find a substitute."

Tabby and I beamed at each other.

"That's the spirit," Tabby said.

I knew keeping my eyes open didn't mean picking locks and getting my friends into heaps of trouble, but how did my dad expect me to find clues if not by taking a few chances? I wasn't about to pass up on the opportunity to help solve a real police case for anything in the world. I'd been waiting for this my whole life and I didn't care about what might happen if we got caught, at least not at that moment.

The bell rang and we had to go to the next two classes. By the time I'd finished PE I felt sure I'd be taking home an injury for the weekend. Edwina kept spiking the volleyball at my head. I felt like crying but I wouldn't give her the satisfaction of letting her see me do that, so I walked off the court all covered in red welts. I felt bullied and I didn't like it at all.

# Chapter Three

"How was Hong Kong?" I asked Mum over Weetabix on Saturday morning.

"Not nearly as exciting as your first week at Hollingsworth, I'll bet." Mum got herself another cup of tea. "You first, and don't leave out any details, Mabel, I want to hear it all. Bernard, where are you, love? Do come and sit down, Mabel's going to tell us about her new friends at Hollingsworth."

"Right there." Dad came into the kitchen in his white short-sleeved shirt, black tie and trousers.

"You're going to work on a Saturday?" I said.

"Just for a bit, love. I've got a case that seems to be picking up. I shan't be long. Now what's this about your new friends, Mabel?" He asked as if he hadn't heard it all before and I really loved him for that. I'm closer to him in a lot of ways. He'd come to get me the evening before and had so many questions I couldn't possibly answer every one.

My dad is thirty-six, with short, very thick black hair. He's clean-shaven and loves to tell stories about adventures he's been on, mostly police raids and helicopter rides, chasing suspects through traffic lights and down motorways. He's very passionate about his work and I think a bit of that's rubbed off on me because I love to hear about how he's solved a case, but he only tells me when he's in a good mood.

"Tell us the best parts," Mum said.

"Tabitha and Hugh came out to meet me on my first day. Tabby's in all my classes and she has a photographic memory."

# The Egyptian Vault

Dad nodded and looked impressed. "Just the sort of company you should be keeping."

"What else?" Mum wore her fluffy pink robe. Her night mask sat up on her forehead and she'd made us sausages and eggs for breakfast.

"Tabby's in the same dorm as I am. She's in the next bed. The other girls are nice enough, but they don't talk to me very much. I suppose it's because I'm the new girl and they're not sure about me yet."

"They'll come around, dear, don't you worry," Mum said.

"Right then, I'm off," Dad kissed us both on our cheeks. "You two keep out of trouble and expect me home for dinner at six."

"Bye, love," Mum turned back to me and sat down taking off her night mask. She put it on the table beside us and took a sip of her tea. She looked at me trying to read my mind it seemed. Sometimes I wonder if she's a bit telepathic, because whenever she calls her sister in London it's always exactly when something serious has happened, such as she's lost her job or been in a car accident.

Mum is older than her sister, and slimmer, with long thick dark hair she often ties up in a bun. She has very large green eyes, and always plucks her eyebrows because she says if she didn't they would grow together. I think she's beautiful and I don't look a thing like her. Her smile makes you think she ought to be in a toothpaste ad.

"From the sound of it, you're lucky to have met Tabitha and Hugh on your first day."

"They're terrific. Tabby and I were talking about getting together this weekend. Would you mind if I did?"

Mum looked disappointed, I suppose because she wanted to have me all to herself, but I wanted to talk to Tabby about our plans for getting our hands on the diary.

"Why don't you give her a call and we'll run you over there tomorrow afternoon?"

I could tell I'd hurt her feelings and to make it up to her, I gave her some more details.

"The Matron seems very nice too. Her name is Elise, but we have to call her Matron Dorsett. Tabby says that if ever we have a nosebleed or hurt ourselves, we're to go straight to her room across from the sick bay."

"Sick bay? What's that?" Mum asked.

"The place boarders go when they're sick and there's no one nearby to come and fetch them."

"And Mr. Pearson, what's he like?"

"I'm not sure yet. He did come and introduce himself on my first day. He gave us a lecture at assembly and said he expects us all to respect each other. We're not to dye our hair or get tattoos or any piercings, and tropical beads are strictly out! You know, normal type stuff."

I showed Mum my *History of Art* book. As humiliated as I'd felt on my first meeting with Mr. Reeves, I still liked the class. There was a paper sticking out between the pages and I opened it thinking I must have left some notes inside, but instead I read:

"JUST LOOKING AT YOU GIVES ME A RASH, CHARITY CASE. XOXO EC"

# The Egyptian Vault

"What's that?" I could feel tears start to burn my eyes. I didn't want to show Mum because I wanted her to believe that the week at school really had gone smoothly.

"A note from a horrid girl who hates me. She's a bully."

Then Mum read the note. "We've got to do something. We can't have girls getting away with this sort of thing."

"She pinched me and I think it's all because of the scholarship."

"I'll ring her parents and sort this out right away."

"Please don't. It will only make things worse. Maybe she'll give up. Tabby says she's from a rich family and they're all beastly. She's a spoiled brat and walks about as if she owns the school."

"I'm so sorry, Mabel." Mum hugged me. "I never expected you to have to deal with this sort of thing. You know, if this persists, we'll have to go to Mr. Pearson."

"I'll tell you if something else happens."

"Do you promise?" Mum said.

"Promise."

She kissed me on the top of my head. "We have to look out for each other, don't we? Now, why don't you go and ring Tabby? I have to get in the shower. Perhaps we'll leave the dishes for Dad."

I put my plate in the sink and heard her go up the stairs. Then I looked down the hall. Dad had left the door to his office open! When I got there, I saw papers scattered on his desk. The curtains were still drawn half way across the windows.

A window seat looked out onto Captain's Row and all kinds of people were walking to and from the High Street. On the red velvet armchairs in front of the desk, our two cats, Finnegan and James, both looked up at me with their Siamese chocolate faces, ice-blue eyes and tan bodies.

Dad's briefcase lay open on the desk, and as quickly as I could I found the folder marked *Stolen Paintings*. I opened the file and right at the very top I saw a paper with the name *Henry Corrigan* and *Bowler's Green Auction House and Gallery*. That had to be Edwina's dad, and then in my dad's scribbles I read *Forgeries?* And the date of his interview, which had been October 1, 1980.

No wonder Edwina hated me, especially if she knew that a police file had been opened with her dad's name on it.

I heard the water going in the shower upstairs. I felt safe for a few more minutes. Flipping through the pages, I came across a page dated 1923 from the Paris Police. They'd been investigating the Hollingsworth Estate and had talked to someone called Neville Hollingsworth about stolen paintings.

Underneath I found what looked like a small stack of building blueprints. I prayed for paper in Dad's copy machine, checked it and felt relieved. I picked up the papers in the whole file and began to copy everything. My heart thundered like piano keys in my chest.

I told myself to breathe and concentrate. I laid out the blueprints and minimized them to fit on one page; then I heard the sound of the water going off. The last paper floated into the copy tray below. I put the papers back and bolted. I dashed up the stairs, knowing Mum would be coming out any moment. I closed my bedroom door and heard her walking along the floorboards towards my room.

"Have you spoken to Tabitha yet?"

"No, not yet."

"You need to, Mabel. Let's do a bit of shopping. Anything you need, love?"

"Nothing I can think of right now."

"Well, make a list then."

"Shall do." I looked around my room for a hiding place. The knob on the top of my bedpost had come loose the week before. Dad would never think of looking in there. Perfect! I rolled the papers up, stuffed them down inside, and put the knob back on top. Then I sat on my bed for a minute trying to imagine why Dad hadn't taken his briefcase and his files with him to work. Maybe he really did need my help in solving the case but didn't know how to give me the information. That made sense.

Before we left the house to go shopping, I remembered to call Tabby. She explained to me how to get to her house. I didn't know what she'd make of the file and I felt a bit scared of what I'd just done, but I didn't regret it for a moment.

We spent the rest of the afternoon at Lymington Market, just steps from our door. The market is held every Saturday and takes up the entire High Street. I tried to have fun with Mum but all I could think of were the papers in my bedpost.

+++

The next day we drove to Tabby's house in the heart of the New Forest. It's one of my favourite places on earth. Wild horses run free there and you feel like Robin Hood himself might pop out from behind the trees and hand you a bag of gold.

"What did you say her father did again, Mabel?" Dad asked me.

"I think he's in real estate."

I knew Mum had always wanted a proper house with a garden and reception rooms, and as we pulled up the circular drive, I could see that what she'd been dreaming of was a house like Tabby's, with ivy growing up every wall. Dad pulled to a halt by the stone lions that stood on either side of the front path.

"Thanks." I opened the car door. "Could you come back and collect me at about five, please"

"Of course we can," Mum said.

I'd brought my textbook and Edwina's horrid note to show Tabby and had taken the papers out of my bed rail and put them inside the book too.

Before I had even climbed the first step, Tabby opened the door and pulled me inside.

"I can't believe you got the stuff so quickly. Come in, come in. We can get something to drink and then go straight to my room."

A woman in a fawn jumper and plaid skirt appeared from the hall. She looked frail and moved as if she was aching all over. She had a shawl wrapped around her shoulders and had the same freckly skin as Tabitha, but that was where the resemblance ended.

Tabitha introduced us and I went over to shake her hand, but she looked quite uncomfortable at that and I wondered if I'd done something wrong. Then she said, "My congratulations on winning the scholarship, Mabel. Tabitha's told me all about you.

Please make yourself at home. I'll be in the study if you need me."

"She's always in the study under a blanket on the sofa. She never budges." Tabby took me into the kitchen and got us some soft drinks and crisps. "It's a big worry. The doctors say she's afraid of open spaces, so leaving the house is out of the question for her. She never goes anywhere and doesn't want anyone to come in."

"Has she always been like this?" I asked.

"You mean afraid of her own shadow? More so in the last few years. It's been getting worse though and Dad doesn't know what to do, neither do I. She used to be loads of fun, but now she just hides away in there."

"Is she going to be all right?"

"I hope so."

"Sounds hard."

"It is, but enough about that. Now you tell me what you've found out."

I whispered very softly and beckoned her to come closer. "I've copied some of my dad's police files."

"You didn't! Isn't that against the law?"

"No, only if you get caught. Does that change things for you?"

"I wouldn't dream of being left out of this," Tabby said with relish. "And besides, it will keep school interesting and no one has to find out, do they?"

"No one is going to find out, I promise you that."

"Let's go upstairs before you breathe another word and my dad finds out you've come."

"Don't you want him to know I'm here?" I felt a little hurt.

"Oh, you have nothing to do with it. If he catches us, he'll take over the visit and you'll spend the whole time with him in his library talking about French colonies. That's what really gets him going and you'll never hear the end of it. He *loves* an audience."

I smiled to myself thinking at least Tabby came by it honestly.

Tabby led me up the poshest staircase I'd ever seen, with a large winding wood banister and a huge crystal chandelier above us. Just as we got to the top step we heard someone below.

"Tabitha, Tabitha."

"I knew we might not make it." She looked over the railing and down to the foyer.

"Dad, we looked for you. Mabel's here. Say hello." She nudged me and whispered, "Be quick and we might make a break for it."

"Hello Mr. Mason, how nice to meet you."

I could see Tabby's father on the bottom step fighting the urge to come up.

"Enjoying Hollingsworth, are you, Mabel?"

"Very much."

"We're going to be in my room if that's all right?" Tabby asked.

"Fine, fine, we might see you later." Mr. Mason had long red sideburns that formed a sort of a beard around his chin. He had very little in the way of hair on the top of his head but his face looked as if it was permanently red.

"Perhaps we'll see you before you go, Mabel. Tab's told us so much about you."

"Come on, quick," she waved and I followed her into her room.

# The Egyptian Vault

"He seems kind."

"When he's here, he's good, interested and all that, but he gets called out so often that sometimes I don't see him at weekends as he's always going to show this house or make an offer on another. A slave to his clients he is. Has to do whatever they want at a moment's notice."

"Doesn't he ever come to school to see you for lunch?"

"Never, nobody's parents do. It's like when we're gone, they're pleased to have the house to themselves. But enough of that, now you tell me everything."

Looking around, I saw that Tabby had a bedroom made for a princess. It had a wall of windows and a four-poster bed with pink curtains. Shelves of books surrounded a window seat and ponies grazed in the field behind the house.

"Don't mind my room. I'd never get anything this fancy for myself, but as I'm the only girl, Mum fusses over me. Go on then, I can barely wait another second."

I showed her the papers.

"Any idea who these paintings are by?"

"Someone called Marc Chagall. Have you ever heard of him?"

"Mabel! He's *world* famous, right up there with Van Gogh and Picasso. He's sublime."

She flopped onto her bed and laughed. "I knew you were trouble from the first moment I saw you. But this is far more than I could have imagined."

She looked serious for a minute with her head propped up on her elbow. "But what would his paintings be doing at our school?"

## The Egyptian Vault

I ran and jumped onto the bed beside her. "That's what we're going to find out."

# The Egyptian Vault

# Chapter Four

At breakfast next morning we told Hugh what I'd done. "Are you mad? You could get arrested or something."

"My dad's not going to arrest me! Besides, I think he left the files out there deliberately for me to see."

"Why do you say that?" Hugh asked.

"Because he's never left the door open before and he went off to work without his briefcase, leaving the file on the paintings *right* there on his desk. He must have known I'd look. But he's probably not allowed to tell anyone he's passing information to me."

"Sounds like you're a family of spies," Hugh chuckled.

"He's never been like this before," I said quite seriously. "He must really want to solve this case. He never forgets anything, especially locking the door to his study."

I thought about all the times he'd caught me trying to pick the lock on his briefcase but there wasn't much point talking about that right now.

"This is probably more than you bargained for?" I looked at him hoping I hadn't scared him off.

"Don't get me wrong, I'm still in," he said. "I need a little more time to think about this. That's all. I don't want you to have to leave the school, Mabel."

"I'm not going anywhere. We have a case to solve and I can't do it without both of you helping. Shall we meet in the library at lunch and then have

31

a go at the glass case? I've brought some hair pins. They work best."

"It sounds like you want to be the leader of our group," Tabby said. I couldn't be sure what she was thinking.

"Sorry, sometimes I can be bossy especially when I get excited about something. I don't mean to be."

"Oh, don't get me wrong," Tabby said. "I'd hate to be the leader and besides you're a natural, really you are."

I looked over at Hugh.

"Mabel," he smiled, "I think you're the only one that wants the job."

+++

By the time we got to lunch even I was starting to get nervous. We chose a table close to the door, ate quickly, and piled our trays on the way out hoping no one would notice we'd left early. Once we got to the library we barely spoke to each other. We made our way quietly to the glass cabinet and looked at it for a few seconds.

"Has anyone seen Ms. Asquith?" Hugh asked.

"She went out just a few minutes before we came in. I saw her going down to lunch. Now are you sure you can do this, Mabel?" Tabby asked.

What a pity we didn't look to see if anyone had come in after us. We just assumed we had the place to ourselves.

"I found a book we can use as a substitute." Hugh took a burgundy leather notebook from his bag. "One of my dad's old school books from up in the attic. I wrote her name on the front cover for good measure. Should do the job, don't you think?"

# The Egyptian Vault

Comparing the two, I saw they were almost identical. My heart started to race, which I took as a good sign. I reached for the hairgrips in my pocket and found one that I shaped into an L. I inserted that one into the hole at the bottom of the padlock and then I put another one into the lock, just a bit further up inside the keyhole. I began to jiggle the second hairgrip gently, because that's how I'd managed to open my "test" locks at home.

After a few minutes, I could barely stand it. I felt sure we'd be found out, but then something clicked inside and the lock opened. I lifted the glass lid and motioned for Hugh to hand me the substitute while I reached for Emily's diary.

Briefly, I imagined Mr. Pearson appearing behind us. I could hear him saying, "We should never have let you into our school, Mabel Hartley; you're a common thief."

I put the diary in my bag and placed Hugh's book inside the cabinet. I couldn't finish soon enough. We all started for the exit.

"Why don't we go to the stables?" Hugh said. "We've got half an hour, and no one will be in there. It might give us a chance to have a look without anyone pestering us."

"Stables it is," I said.

We ran across the footbridge and down the front steps. We turned the corner and walked as quickly as we could by the arches along the front of the school and into the interior courtyard. The wooden door to the stables felt heavy, planked and rough. Tabby thought it would be open, but today we found the latch closed, which meant that no one was inside. Pupils could enter the stables at any time, as many groomed their horses after dinner and at lunchtime.

"Looks as if we're the only ones here." Tabby walked past the horses in the stables on either side of us. Once we'd passed the fifth set of stables we came to a dark, musty tackle room.

Inside a cage, a white rabbit sat on a hay bale. She had pink eyes and stared at me while she sucked from a water bottle. Saddles, bridles, and horse blankets hung from the walls. I felt safe but I wished that I'd brought a few carrots for the horses to munch on.

"Diary or case files first?" I asked.

"Diary," Tabby and Hugh said together.

I took the diary out of my bag, and the three of us sat down on the hay bales. I opened the front cover. Something made me hesitate.

"I think we should make a pact," I said.

"What sort of a pact?" Tabby wondered.

"That we only read the diary when we're together, so we won't be as likely to get caught by the powers that be."

"Not a bad idea," Hugh said.

"Shouldn't we prick our fingers and seal it with blood or something?" Tabby asked earnestly.

"That's not *really* necessary, is it?" Hugh crinkled up his face.

"No, must we really, Tabby?"

"I suppose not, but it's what they do in the books, isn't it? What shall we do then, swear an oath?"

"I would," I nodded. "Tell us what to say."

"We'll start by joining hands in a circle." I liked the idea already and reached for Hugh's hand. It

34

felt warm and soft against mine. I'd never held a boy's hand before. I looked at Tabby wondering if she knew how grateful I was for her hare-brained schemes, but her eyes were shut tight.

"It should start with us all saying, "I do solemnly swear, repeat after me," Tabby said. "On all that I hold dear, never to forsake this bond."

Hugh rolled his eyes but repeated after Tabby.

"Yes, never to forsake this bond, and if any one of us breaks the seal, of God and country, may we fall into a quagmire of such ponderous calamity that our sons and brothers will be doomed forever after." Tabby squeezed my hand and opened her eyes. "That's all. Now, go ahead, Mabel."

The diary felt like a napkin in my hand. I looked inside. Emily's ladylike handwriting looked loopy. I read:

*This book belongs to Emily Iris Hollingsworth,*
*Hollingsworth Estate, Milford-on-Sea, 1909*
*February 1909*
*I am starting this diary because today is my birthday and I am now seventeen years of age. I expected father at breakfast, perhaps with a card, and some flowers he likes to pick from the garden, but it is already afternoon and I have not yet seen him. I fear he has forgotten me altogether. Nellie has suggested that he may be busy with his research in his study and that he is certain to appear momentarily, but this is not the first time he's forgotten my special day.*

*I shall content myself therefore with a walk in the garden. It makes me miss my mother. Seven years have passed since she died and still I cannot believe she is gone. It is such a cross to bear.*

*Father promised to take a greater interest and sometimes he does but only when he needs to take a pause from his work. Occasionally we have tea together. I've not a friend in the world save Nellie, my chambermaid. I find myself wishing my birthday were already over, so that my disappointment might end tonight.*

*Tomorrow will be a new day, and a new year in my life. I fear I shall never leave Hollingsworth or see anything of the world. Instead I shall be forgotten here like an old spinster. This is a sad day for me and a tragic beginning to this diary. I shall write more soon.*

"She sounds so melancholy," Tabby said, "Like a typical heiress though. Wealthy beyond comparison and saddled with loneliness."

"Nothing about the paintings, so maybe it's a dead end after all." I felt out of sorts myself. I never thought I'd have anything in common with an heiress, but Mum had been away for many of my birthdays too, and I'd get a kiss in the morning from Dad, but with no company the day usually dragged on forever.

We heard the sound of voices entering the stables, and I shut the diary with a start.

"Father says I deserve a new pony, and I have to agree with him."

"It's Edwina!" Tabby bobbed up and looked over to the entrance of the stables. "Keep it out of sight," she motioned to the diary.

"What's she doing in here?" I stuffed the diary into my bag.

# The Egyptian Vault

"Three of the ponies are hers," Hugh whispered and we all backed into the nearest corner and crouched down.

"But Mr. Pearson has said that I can only keep three here at the school, so Father said he'd have a chat with him."

"To think we have to share the stables with the rest of the school, it's criminal really." Another voice said, "It's hardly fair! All our money is going to support the charity cases."

"Did you see her hair?" Edwina sniggered. "She's positively a beast that's crawled out from beneath a rock. I wish she'd go back there. She's company even the horses won't tolerate. Let's go and see if we can find *little* Mabel."

We heard the door shut and they were gone.

"Who was the other girl?" I asked.

"Tara Bhatti," Tabby said, "and she's just like her name sounds, crazy. Both are rotten to the core. They're gone now; how about we take a look at the papers from your dad's desk?"

I knew she was trying to be kind by changing the subject but I couldn't help thinking how horrid those girls were and now I knew why they had it in for me. Tabby put an arm around my shoulder.

"Mabel, tell Hugh what you've found. I promise that will make you feel better."

"It seems to me that there are really two cases in this file." I felt sufficiently cheered up. "Here, let's spread them out on the floor so we can have a better look. Yesterday, we read that the paintings my dad is looking for are by an artist called Marc Chagall."

# The Egyptian Vault

"I think he's here in our *History of Art* book." Hugh got his bag out. "I was trying to get ahead of Mr. Reeves so I was leafing through it over the weekend, so I could surprise him with my vast knowledge."

"I don't think Mr. Reeves would ever let on he was impressed," Tabby said.

"You're probably right. Here he is. Take a look at this painting. It's bizarre, all topsy-turvy, people floating through the sky and nothing quite what it looks like in real life, very dreamlike. This one is called *A Sapphire Moon*. He tried to recreate it after he lost the original in Paris during the First World War. There's a bit about his extreme use of vibrant colour, and how he's one of those Expressionist painters, but in the Fauves group, whatever that means."

I took the book and looked closely at the blue painting, the colour of violet flowers you see in the garden or how the sky looks just before night sets in. I could see a white moon rising in the sky above Notre Dame Cathedral, and a bride and groom floating in the sky. Above them, I saw a white cockerel and a green goat that looked serene and bizarre at one and the same time.

"If the paintings did come to the estate, where could they be hidden? There must be a thousand different places," I said.

"Didn't you say there were blueprints in here?" Tabby asked.

I took the copies I'd made out of the file. "I could never be an architect," I said. "This makes no sense. I can't even make out what building this one is from."

# The Egyptian Vault

"Perhaps because it's upside down," Hugh said. "Turn it this way and I think you have the main part of the house with all the dorms. Right here is your Cartoon Gallery, and your room is there." Hugh tapped the drawing with his finger.

"How did you know that?" I asked.

"It's a boy thing," Tabby said. "They all have the genes for making sense of drawings and mechanics that look like squiggles to us."

"This is your room and down here is the Matron's office, and the sick bay," and then he stopped.

"What is it?" Tabby said.

"I'm not sure," Hugh said. "By the look of things there's a whole other wing on the house here behind the wall in the sick bay." We all stared at the lines and then I could see other rooms quite plainly.

"What would that area be?" Tabby said.

"Somewhere to hide paintings," Hugh said, "if you knew how to get in there."

"Do you think there are others who know about this?" I asked.

"Such as who?" Tabby said.

"The staff."

"Not unless they've studied these drawings," Hugh said. "No one would ever know unless they had a copy of this. What's the other case your dad's working on? How does it tie into this?"

"It's about the *Bowler's Green Auction House* and a connection to a fake Chagall called *Girl with the Goat*," I said.

"The textbook here says that a real Chagall could be worth millions now."

"Millions?" Tabby and I said together.

"Millions," Hugh said.

We heard the bell go, and packed up.

+++

Next morning in the History of Art class, Edwina arrived a little late with a drink in her hand. She came around behind me, leaned forward and poured it into my bag.

"Edwina, what on earth are you doing?" Mr. Reeves said.

"Sorry, Mabel. Did I get your bag? I must have tripped," she said with a smile.

Tabby grabbed my arm, and whispered, "Diary? Papers? Tell me they're not in your bag, are they?"

"No, Hugh's got them."

Mr. Reeves charged over.

"It was an accident," Edwina said. "An accident."

"Well you can expect to pay for her bag and everything in it, accident or not," Mr. Reeves said.

"What do you mean? I'll have to replace everything in Mabel's bag?" She stopped for a second before she sat down and said loudly, "Yes, I get it. It's because she doesn't have the money to buy her own things. Yes, I understand completely, now; charity cases get special treatment."

I felt my face start to burn.

"You go to the Headmaster's Office at once, Edwina, and take Mabel's bag with you. Be sure to clean it up as best you can. Tell him what you've told me; I'll be surprised if you're back in here before next week."

As he dismissed her and turned back toward the centre of the room, Edwina pinched me even harder than before. "I shan't forget this, Mabel, you mark my words."

# The Egyptian Vault

"We'll find a way to get back at her," Tabby said, "and when we do, she'll regret the day she set eyes on you."

"Your attention, please," Mr. Reeves was saying, "During the next few weeks we'll be exploring the differences between artistic movements by doing weekly demonstrations in class. Please be ready to bring your sketchbooks to class. You will be marked on your renditions."

"Is he going to be doing the demos?" Tabby whispered.

"It sounds like it," I said.

"Who ever thought he could paint?" Hugh asked.

Within minutes Mr. Reeves had set up an easel at the front of the class, had taken his paints out and had begun preparing the colours on his palette, "We'll start with Monet and his famous Water Lilies. This one will be for your benefit, Mabel Hartley. You can take this one home and practise your technique."

I thought I saw him smile at me and then he winked. When Hugh had carried my bag up the front steps on my first day, he'd winked at me too and I couldn't help but smile.

+++

I knew that Edwina hated me, but I didn't realize how much until we got to our dorm after dinner. Above my bed she'd scrawled CHARITY CASE in large letters in red paint.

"Mr. Pearson ought to see this," I said thinking about the promise I'd made to my mum. "I thought she was going to be sent home."

On the floor beside my bed I noticed my bag in a puddle of liquid.

"Not soon enough, obviously!" Tabby said.

Matron Dorsett appeared in the doorway dressed in her white coat and black orthopaedic shoes, a statuesque woman with brown hair and large features, her hair parted in the middle and feathered down to her shoulders. In the right light, she easily could pass for a man, because she has a meaty kind of face. She came and sat on the bed and took my hand.

"Bullying happens to everyone at some point. I'm just so very sorry you've become a victim of it so soon."

"Edwina Corrigan did this," Tabby said.

"Well, do you have any proof of that?" Matron asked.

"Mr. Reeves knows all about it," Tabby said.

"I see," Matron said. "Mabel, will you trust me to make this right for you?"

"Yes," I said meekly.

"Good. Now you leave this to me. Tabby, I'd like you to take Mabel to the stables, and show her the horses; that will be nice and soothing. Then come back and have a nice bath and it will be all cleared up, but not before I show Mr. Pearson."

True to her word, the scrawled red words were gone by the time we returned, and my bag had been washed, turned inside out and left to hang dry. Matron also left a note on my bedside table that said Mr. Pearson wanted to see me in the morning, with Hugh and Tabitha. For some reason that made me feel even worse.

The Egyptian Vault

# Chapter Five

The next morning was the first day of November. The three of us were sitting outside Mr. Pearson's office reading Emily's diary, which we'd put between the covers of my History of Art textbook.

"I'm not sure about reading the diary here," Tabby said. "You do realize we are outside the headmaster's office? If he catches us, we'll all be expelled."

"He's not going to notice," I said. "We'll close the book as soon as he comes out, I promise. But we need to keep reading. We're off to the Tate and we can't possibly bring it on the bus, especially with Edwina lurking about."

"I think we should stop talking and start reading," Hugh said. "He's not supposed to come out for at least another five minutes. Where did we get to?"

*Life has improved tremendously since my last entry. My birthday was a bore, as it always is, so I should not be disappointed. This time, however, Father has more than made it up to me, because painters have arrived and they are young and French!*

*Father said it was high time that we finished his dining room upstairs, and that he needed a mural to complete the room or it would always feel unfinished in his eyes. He also says that bringing in locals is just asking for trouble, because when people are a bit queer (as we are) the word gets around.*

*Father is frightened lest someone find out what he's been doing under the library, and to normal people who know little about Egypt and how much Father has invested in his work, they might think twice about getting to know us.*

*I know that he's thinking of my marriage and arranging it with another family of means, and that the peculiar aspects of our estate might not be perceived in the best light. But I know that I must marry for love because why else would one do it?*

*I have asked Father if he loved Mother, and he said, "Of course Emily, I adored her, but we grew to love each other, just as you will grow to love your husband, when we find one who is suitable."*

*The painters have been here for a few weeks now and I only see them going down the stairs for dinner, as Father does not permit them to eat with us. He says that in matters of propriety, they must eat with the servants.*

*Nellie, my chambermaid, has told me that one of the painters has been asking about me. His name is Gustave and she says he is only twenty years old, but that he has the most wonderful sense of humour. He told her he would like to play the organ (you know where) and she said she would ask me about it.*

*Last night, we were on the other side, and he began to play for us. He kept looking back at me. We laughed and laughed. During the daytime now I can practise my French with him. Tell me, dear diary, what am I to do with this boy? My affection for him grows. I shall write again soon, your Emily.*

We were so engrossed in the diary that none of us heard Mr. Pearson clear his throat. I snapped the book shut and he led us into his office, none the wiser, or so I hoped.

# The Egyptian Vault

"Please sit down." He went around behind his desk.

"Let me start by offering you an apology, Mabel, for the graffiti above your bed. I am disturbed to say the least." He shuffled some papers on his desk. "I understand the three of you have become quite close these last few weeks."

I couldn't think of anything to say, so I nodded, but Tabby piped up, "Edwina has got it in for Mabel, Sir. We overheard her yesterday being beastly about Mabel and then she poured her drink into Mabel's bag. The graffiti was the ultimate insult."

Mr. Pearson sat up in his chair and stretched his hands across the desk. He looked almost like a circus trainer, less the bow tie and tails, but I thought the roles were the same – cajoling wild animals to perform parlour tricks. I could see he took the matter very seriously. He'd slicked back his thick blond hair with a comb that left tooth lines. His perfectly manicured hands gave an air of greater wealth than any of us could imagine.

Behind his desk, in fact around the whole room, were portraits of men, all sitting with dogs at their feet, in ties and suits with black robes on. I wondered if they'd ever asked a woman to sit for a portrait. Probably not.

"Who are all the men in these portraits?" I asked.

"Former headmasters." Mr. Pearson relaxed leaning back in his chair. "Except for this one." He motioned to the one portrait that hung on the wall behind his desk. "This is Neville Hollingsworth, the brother of Edmond Hollingsworth, who lived here for a number of years. After Edmond died, Neville

45

assumed responsibility for the property, and brought his son Caleb with him. After their time here the estate was bought privately and in 1945 was turned into this school."

In the portrait, Neville wore a naval uniform with gilded buttons and sleeves, and a Napoleon-style hat. A belt with a long sword slung off his hip.

"What happened to him?" Hugh asked.

"One day he walked off the estate and never came back. It's a pity really, because from what I know a finer man could not have been found." Mr. Pearson turned to admire the portrait again.

When he had his back turned to us, Tabitha leaned over and whispered to me, "Neville's just been put up there. Every time I've been in here before, he's never been there."

"What were you in here for?" I whispered back.

"To see about you."

"Me?"

"Welcoming you, that's all." Tabby gave my arm a light squeeze.

"In any case," Mr. Pearson continued, "we're here to talk about Mabel."

"We all know Edwina did it," Tabby said.

"We need to be sure, Tabitha. Mabel, it's actually you I'd like to hear from."

"She's made me think about whether I can carry on here." The way I said it certainly sounded as if I had every intention of leaving but I hadn't said as much to Tabby and Hugh.

Mr. Pearson leaned his elbows on his desk and sighed. I knew my words were having the desired effect.

# The Egyptian Vault

"She left this note in my textbook after she pinched me in class."

"May I see the note?" he asked.

I reached into my bag, took my textbook out, and passed the note to Mr. Pearson.

"I think she's dangerous, and I'm afraid of her. In her mind there's no room for people like me here."

"People like you?" Mr. Pearson said.

"Yes, people that don't come from - how shall I say it? - the moneyed classes."

"I shall have Mr. Reeves assign her a new seat in your History of Art class, and I shall personally speak to her again about this matter. We shall have this settled before the week is through. Tabitha and Hugh, I charge you with keeping an eye on Mabel and reporting to me the slightest sign of any further behavior of this sort. That will be all."

"Leaving didn't really cross your mind, did it?" Tabby asked when we'd walked outside the hall.

"No, of course not, but I thought it gave just the right effect."

"Not to worry, Mabel, we'll protect you." Hugh put his arm around my shoulder. "Even Mr. Pearson's on our side. Now let's find the bus we're supposed to be on or Mr. Reeves might leave without us."

+++

We boarded the bus last, making sure to find seats as far from Edwina as possible. She was sitting near the back, so we sat as close to the driver as we could. It took us an hour to reach London and Mr. Reeves passed egg sandwiches around telling us to eat them on the bus and not to set foot in the Tate with food in our bags. It's not every day you get to go to the National Gallery of British Art.

In the parking lot, I wondered if Emily Hollingsworth might have come here. The grand portico entrance felt awe-inspiring and the central dome inside made it seem like a palace.

Mr. Reeves directed us into one of the Impressionist wings and then he ran into someone wearing a black bowler hat and a long grey coat. They shook hands and then the other man took off his hat and held it with brown leather gloves on a walking stick. They seemed very familiar with one another.

I heard Edwina say, "Daddy!" and my stomach turned.

Mr. Reeves told us all to queue up at the help desk to collect our headphones for the tour and then he and Edwina's father went off into the wing next to ours. He didn't come back for a long time.

After we picked up our headsets, we started the tour and heard a lot about the earliest British painters, who, in my opinion, were a great bunch of bores. I really didn't want to listen to anything about them, because all they painted was farmers' fields, rivers and churches, and I'd certainly had enough of those.

What I wanted was colour, and light and more Impressionists, and perhaps we'd even get to see a Chagall or two. At one point Tabitha took off her headphones and said she'd fast-forwarded her tape to the Chagall part, and that we should head to the gallery with the Van Goghs because Chagall was sure to be right around the corner from him.

# The Egyptian Vault

After Van Gogh had played through on the headset, the voice started to talk about Picasso, and the Cubist movement.

*New painting styles were emerging in the early 20th century; art patrons and dealers revolved around them. Marc Chagall stayed true to his own vision and earliest inspiration despite Picasso's influence. Born in Russia in 1887, Moshe Shagal lived in the city of Vitebsk.*

I stopped and stood in front of the great Chagall masterpiece, *Bouquet with Flying Lovers*. A huge bouquet of flowers dominated the otherwise blue canvas. A woman flew above the flowers with a man beside her. My heart felt lighter looking at her and below the couple I could see a bridge with arches on the left and below it, a little man in a rowing boat.

*The first of nine children in a Hasidic Jewish family, Chagall's mother Feiga-Ita bribed the teacher to enrol Moshe in the local public school, which prohibited Jews. His grandfather had been a rabbi while his father worked as a herring vendor. Chagall claimed never to have seen a painting until 1906 when he decided to become an artist.*

*Joining a local art school, Chagall painted in purple. It seemed so bold that from then on they gave him free tuition because of his unique skill. In 1907, he set out for St. Petersburg where he met his fiancé, Bella, in 1909.*

As much as I loved hearing about Chagall, I needed a break, so I found Tabby and Hugh and we went to sit at a bench in front of some more Chagall paintings.

# The Egyptian Vault

"Imagine if we found the paintings," Tabby said. "They might hang them here one day, beside these ones."

Mr. Reeves joined us again, now without Mr. Corrigan. I looked about, but I couldn't see Edwina and I hoped she'd left with her father. I think Mr. Reeves thought we were all still listening to the headsets because he went and stood by himself in front of the *Bouquet with Flying Lovers.*

+++

When we returned to school, we found out that we'd all been assigned to activity clubs, mostly because, as Tabby said, the teachers wanted us to get more fresh air. Half the school lined up in the foyer to get a look at the lists for the clubs. I remembered how I'd put down rowing as an interest on my student profile. Apparently, so had Tabby and Hugh but Edwina had been assigned as our coach.

"This has got to be a joke," Hugh said.

"We can't possibly spend the afternoon with her and why does she get to be the coach? It must have been decided before the graffiti," Tabby said.

My heart sank.

"Don't worry," Tabby said. "We just won't go. We'll say that you weren't feeling well."

"We can't all say that," Hugh said.

"Why don't we go and talk to Mr. Pearson?" Tabby said. "He's right over there coming out of his office. Mr. Pearson, Mr. Pearson!" Tabby took the notice off the board and went to show him. "May we have a minute? We've been put in the rowing club with Edwina! Can you give us special permission to join another club instead, please?"

# The Egyptian Vault

"The clubs are out of my hands," Mr. Pearson closed the door to his office. "But I can assure you that Edwina won't be bothering you anymore. I had words with her this morning and she is well aware of the gravity of the situation and what the consequences will be if she bothers you again."

"But she hates Mabel," Tabby said.

"Hate is a very strong word, Tabitha," Mr. Pearson glared at her. "Now go along and if there's any trouble then we'll see about putting you all in another club."

"I can't believe this." Tabby scrunched the notice up into a ball and threw it in the rubbish.

"I'm sure he's right," I said. "She won't do anything more, will she?"

The three of us decided to arrive a little late so as to blend in a bit, but as soon as she saw me Edwina called me up to the front of the pier.

"Right, Mabel, you stay right here. You'll do best as a coxswain and that means you'll be sitting in the stern of the boat. Now I've been encouraged to make friends with you and that's what I'm going to do. Everyone else, would you go and fetch the boats, please? And please make it quick."

Tabby and Hugh looked at me and then at each other.

"Go on, Tabby and Hugh," Edwina said. "Mabel will be fine with me here."

"What do you take us for?" Tabby said. "Mr. Pearson told us to protect her from you. We're not going anywhere, are we Hugh?"

"You'll go where you're told to, Tabby, because I'm the one in charge here. I don't see Mr. Pearson on this dock and besides, Mabel and I have a new understanding, don't we, Mabel?"

I looked at Tabby. Everyone stared at us.

"Go on, I'll be fine, Tabby. Get the boats out and we'll have a practice."

I wanted to give Edwina a chance to make it up to me. I wanted to belong and for once in my life I decided to ignore my intuition and hope Edwina would act in an honourable way. But once they were out of earshot she grabbed my arm above the elbow and said, "Mabel, do you fancy a swim?"

"What? Now?" I said. "It's November, Edwina. You must be mad."

"Mad?" she said, and I knew I'd said completely the wrong thing because then she smiled menacingly and said, "Do you see that little rock pointing up out of the water, just there? Well, I fancy with a little help you could reach it."

Before anyone could get back to us, she gave me a big push off the dock, and sent me flying into the water with my arms pin-wheeling, as I tried to catch my balance. I fell in head first and I must have turned a bit away from her because all I saw was the rock heading straight for my head before I passed out.

I don't remember it at all, but Tabby said Hugh jumped in first and swam out to me. He lifted me onto the dock and I started to cough. Water came up out of my lungs and Tabitha knelt on the dock beside me.

"Do you think I should do mouth to mouth?" she asked Hugh.

"I don't know, Tabby."

# The Egyptian Vault

I blinked and saw Tabitha leaning very closely over me, pulling me onto my side. "That's so the water can come out," she said. "We don't want you to drown lying here."

I could feel something dripping down my face and thought it must just be the water in my hair; then all of a sudden I felt terribly cold.

"We've got to get her inside," Hugh said, "before she gets hypothermia. I'm going to carry you up to sick bay, Mabel. Hold tight."

"Where's Edwina?" I worried she might be circling.

"She's run away." Tabby walked beside us. "She must have realized that finally she's gone too far and now she's hiding. I hope they find her and kick her out."

When we got down to the footbridge, we met Mr. Pearson on the stairs.

"What on earth is going on here?" he asked.

"Edwina pushed Mabel into the lake and, as you can see, Sir, she cut her head open on the rock she hit."

"Where's Edwina now?" he asked.

"Probably trying to arrange for us to get into another club," Tabby said, "now that she's had her fun with poor Mabel."

After that Hugh and Tabby carried me though the front door and up the jaguar staircase past the Cartoon Gallery. They found a bed for me in the sick bay and pulled a blanket up over me. Then they went off to find Matron. A few minutes later she came back with them.

"Mabel Hartley, you certainly have had a rough go of it lately. Let's see to this cut on your forehead." She turned my head gently to one side and pulled back the hair on my temple. Then she used a warm sponge to clean the blood away.

"Bit of a nasty gash. How are you feeling?"

"A bit disoriented."

"That's to be expected, but give me a few minutes and I'll get this sewn up tight for you, just one or two stitches. Now you be a brave girl."

It took ten minutes and I didn't think I'd make it through to the end. Then she asked me to lie down. I didn't want to do anything for a very long time. I think I drifted off to sleep for a while, because when I opened my eyes again, I couldn't see anyone and I felt awfully alone.

# Chapter Six

I would have given anything for a glass of water. I felt like someone had taken an axe to my head. Looking around I saw the sink across the room with a plastic cup beside the tap, so I pulled the covers back and sat up. My head started swimming. Then I remembered the blueprints of this wing of the school.

Behind one of the walls a secret suite of rooms was waiting. I forgot about my head. This chance wouldn't come again. I had to seize it. In spite of everything, I wanted to find the paintings. I pulled myself together, got up and walked the five steps to the sink.

I turned the cold water on and splashed my face. I reached for the towel and then I filled the glass with water and drank it down in one go. I refilled it and drank again. I looked at the door – it was closed – and started to feel better.

Behind me, a wall of beds occupied one part of the room. I looked at the wardrobe by the door and guessed it held linens and supplies for the room. I tried to picture what the room might have been like when Emily lived at Hollingsworth. I imagined it had served many purposes over the years but when did it stop being the entry to the suite? And could we still find the device that opened its door?

I wondered if Mr. Pearson knew about this wing of the school. Looking about I felt frustrated because I didn't have much time. My head began to swim again, and I gripped the sides of the sink, thinking I might faint. I wanted to get back into bed, and looked over my shoulder.

"Only a few more steps, Mabel, and you'll be there!" I told myself.

I started back towards the bed. I must have had a concussion, I thought, because as I walked across the room, something under my feet felt uneven. I tripped and fell hard against the floorboards. Could it be that I was becoming delirious? Then I noticed that one of them had come loose and I pulled myself together and turned around to have a closer look. Someone had cut a portion away from the rest and had reattached it with a separate hinge. I pushed the end down and it sprang back up, revealing a cavity beneath. Inside, a golden crocodile about the length of my palm, with red gleaming eyes, stared up at me.

I reached in to lift it out but when I did, its jaw snapped open. I closed the jaw and then things began to move. The wall with the beds started to turn and then swung around, pivoting on a point somewhere below. I tried to look behind the wall but all I could see was a darkened room. Then the wall slid into place like it had never moved at all.

I snapped the jaws of the crocodile open and shut again. Once more the section of wall began to rotate. I forgot about the pain in my head, got up and moved towards it. The seamless edges gave the illusion of normalcy. I couldn't wait for Tabby and Hugh to come back so I could show them the crocodile and his handy little snapper. But I couldn't be sure how long they'd be and I didn't want to be found out by anyone else. So I put the floorboard back in place and then lay back down on the bed, fighting the urge to snap the jaws once more and go through on my own.

"She's still out." Ten minutes later Tabby opened the door. "Should we wake her up? I don't think people with concussion are supposed to sleep."

"Matron said not to disturb her," Hugh said.

"But what if she's in a coma, and is hooked up to machines for the rest of her life all because we didn't wake her up?"

"Don't be so dramatic. I'm sure she's fine."

Tabitha sat on the edge of my bed and whispered my name.

"Mabel, Mabel." She shook my shoulders. I played dead just to get her going.

"I knew it," she said. "We may never talk to her again.

A smile spread across my face. "You're not rid of me yet." I sat up.

"That was a mean trick!" Tabby said. "I was so worried, wasn't I Hugh, but you probably heard all that, didn't you?"

"How are you feeling, Mabel?" Hugh came over and took my hand and I have to say I loved it. "A bit groggy, but I managed to find the way into the secret suite, and you'll never believe how."

"She's delirious," Tabby looked at me. "Must be because she hit the rock so hard."

"Come and see for yourselves." I pushed myself off the bed swaying a little.

"Easy now," Hugh steadied me.

"No it's right here," I tapped the floorboard with my foot. "Pull the end up, Tabby; it's what's inside that you won't believe."

# The Egyptian Vault

Tabby knelt down with trepidation and pulled at the end of the floorboard. It came back in her hand.

"A crocodile? How very odd." She looked delighted.

"Open and close its jaws."

She did and the wall started to move.

"Come on. We may not have many chances. We have to go in before it closes and that means running across to the other side."

"But you can barely walk." Tabby didn't sound sure at all.

"I'll carry you." Within seconds Hugh swept me into his arms.

"Please let this be all right," Tabby said as the wall shut behind us. "I'm not as fearless as I'd like you all to think."

Once across the threshold, we felt completely cut off from the rest of the school. I tried not to think about that part of the adventure.

The room we'd stepped into had a table full of musical instruments. It looked like a parlour.

"This must have been what Emily mentioned in her last entry, but I haven't got the diary here. I wish there'd been time to bring it."

"I fetched it from your bag when we went to get Matron, just in case," Tabby said.

"We thought it might help but we never imagined you'd find the way to get us in." Hugh took the diary from the inside pocket of his blazer and passed it to me.

"Shall we have a look around and then a quick read?" I took it gratefully. "We don't know how much time we've got."

# The Egyptian Vault

"Is that an organ?" Tabby stepped away from us. "look at the pipes, how they form a bit of a curtain. It's like a confessional booth for organists."

"And here's a gramophone. Aren't they used for playing records? And some kind of tuba." Hugh tried to blow on the mouthpiece and a muffled sound came out.

"There's a lute over here. But you'd never see one of these nowadays: looks like a piano," Tabby sat down on the bench in front of it. "But smaller, and very feminine. I wonder if Emily played it?"

"It's for someone with dainty fingers, and a silk gown, and tiny shoes." I imagined how happy Emily must have been in here.

"Shall we have another look in the diary to see what else she has to say? She might give us a clue about what we're supposed to be looking for," Hugh said.

I opened the diary, but passed it to Tabby because my head hurt too much for me to think of reading.

*1910*

*It is next to impossible to put into words how I have been feeling these last few weeks since Gustave came to the estate. All I can say is that my life has changed completely and Nellie told me I am no long the girl I used to be. I think she is right.*

*For so long I have been waiting for something to happen in my life, and at seventeen I was beginning to give up hope. I must admit I have felt like a prisoner in this house, and with Father gone so much of the time, all I can do is content myself by counting the birds at the birdbath in the garden.*

# The Egyptian Vault

*It seems a hopeless existence for someone like me who has so much energy and nowhere to place it.*

*Gustave has given me an idea of what I can expect to find in the world beyond these walls. He is much older than his years and yet a kindred spirit. One day when I was alone in the garden he addressed me in French, much of which I could understand thanks to having had a French tutor for some years. I felt like a little bird myself, one about to take wing for the first time.*

*He told me of Paris, of his home by the Seine, of his painting, of the food they enjoy there, and how different they are from the "Anglais," as he calls us. He says he has never felt so drawn to anyone and asked if we might go out riding together one day. It seemed rather a bold request, but I could not refuse him nor did I tell Father. We rode out across the fields. I have never prayed for anything so much as for Father to continue his need for painters and for us to have these stolen moments.*

*I showed him some of my sketches and he complimented me on them. He told me I would like the artists he knows at home. I am trying to summon up the nerve to tell Father of our friendship. We have such fun in the music room. Gustave can play all the instruments and even has quite a good voice. He has taken to calling me "The Lady", which I love.*

*Gustave's voice and charm captivate me. He sends me into fits of giggles and now I know he is my best friend.*

"Well she's clearly fallen for him," Tabby said.

# The Egyptian Vault

In the next room was a desk full of cubby-holes, sliding drawers, openings of various sizes, and secret compartments.

"I'll bet you anything this was Emily's father's for all his Egyptian stuff. Look how grand and complex it is. My mum would love one of these desks," Tabby said.

Like the music room, the library had furniture and volumes of books and another desk four drawers high. On top of the desk, portraits and compasses waited to be admired. Beside the desk stood a globe on its own stand, and behind that a little half wall, set between the bookcases. It had all sorts of portraits in oval frames, and a fine chiming clock on a shelf by itself. We saw a ladder beside the wall for climbing up to the top shelves, and a bust of Edmond in the corner by the window.

"There's also a staircase to go upstairs." Tabby came around the corner, and then Hugh peeked his head out beside hers.

"Tabby's right. You need to see this, Mabel, hurry."

At the foot of the banister was a large wooden ball sitting on top of the rail. The staircase led up four flights. At the top was a very dark landing with a small set of rectangular windows running along the top of the wall by the ceiling. Only a few feet wide - a tapestry, of a unicorn surrounded by a fence - hung on the wall.

Looking inside, we guessed from the fine table and chairs that this must have been Edmond Hollingsworth's dining room. The tablecloth had yellowed to the point of being almost brown, and a chandelier with tiny lamps, each with its own lampshade, stood in the middle of the table. Great yellow marble pillars rose around the room. Then we saw the mural of scenes from Egypt: the pyramids, the Sphinx, people riding camels. Gustave's work beyond a doubt. It felt like a ghostly restaurant, with fine red carpets, perhaps from markets in Africa, a huge mirror above the fireplace, and inches of dust covering every surface.

"This is why the painters were in the suite," Hugh said. "But if he was such a recluse, whom did he have over for dinner?"

"No one," I said. "That's why it's so sad. I think he may just have liked the idea of being able to host dinner parties here. What's that over there?"

I saw another door in the wall. I walked over and tried the doorknob, not really sure if it would open or if we would need a key. But the knob turned and I pulled the door toward us. Inside, a platform stretched out over the darkness below, and a wooden staircase went down into the black abyss.

"Hello?" I shouted into the darkness.

"Mabel," Tabby said. "Mind you don't fall."

"I shan't." I stepped back into the dining room, closing the door behind me. "I think we'll find the paintings down there but we'd best leave that for next time."

"Next time!" Tabby said. "I barely had the nerve to come this time. How do you think we're supposed to get out of here?"

"Let's go and see." I took her hand and we walked back down to the music room. All of us were looking around hoping to find a switch that might help us get back into the sick bay.

# The Egyptian Vault

"A-ha!" Hugh found a switch right beside the section of the wall that moved. "Ready?"

"But how do you know it's going to work?" Tabby asked.

"I don't, but it looks like something that might work. Both of you come here beside me and we'll step through. I just hope no one's waiting for us on the other side." Hugh flipped the switch and the wall began to rotate.

"Thank goodness," Tabby said as we rushed through to an empty room. "I didn't want to say anything but I was so worried about being trapped in there and having to escape through the windows on bed sheets. I'm so relieved we didn't have to do that!"

We congratulated ourselves on getting back safely and hoped next time we'd be just as lucky.

+++

Next morning I was ready to present my report on the Expressionists, but Mr. Reeves had other ideas. When we arrived in the classroom he set up a slide projector and said we'd start with a quiz on the paintings we'd seen at the Tate the day before. We all murmured about how unfair it was to surprise us like this, but the thing I noticed first of all was that Edwina was absent, and to me that meant one thing: she'd been expelled and I hoped it was true.

After the quiz, Mr. Reeves asked to see the sketches we'd been working on and he brought out his version of the *Bouquet of Flying Lovers*.

"Students," Mr. Reeves rapped his riding whip against the desk. "Pay attention, please." Then someone came to the door and passed a note to

Mr. Reeves and he nodded in my direction. "You three, down to the headmaster's office at once."

We cleared our books off our desks, walked into the hall and made our way down to the office. "What do you think he wants this time?" Tabby said.

"Must be about Edwina," Hugh said.

We waited on the bench for a few seconds before Mr. Pearson opened the door and called us inside.

"I wanted to tell you all myself that Edwina has been suspended for a week. Matron Dorsett came forward as a witness to the whole event. One other matter, something quite extraordinary came up when I talked to Edwina. Care to venture a guess?"

"I've no idea," I said.

"She said that she saw you take the diary out of the case in the library. I asked Ms. Asquith to verify what she'd said, and apparently the diary is still in the case. Why do you think Edwina might have concocted such a story, Mabel?"

I looked at him. "Probably because she's had it in for me all along. And I have to say that I'm a bit surprised you would believe anything she says at this point."

"Yes, well, I just thought I'd ask."

"You have asked," Tabby said. "Now why don't you leave Mabel alone and expel Edwina for good. Maybe all you really do care about is rich girls and what their parents think."

"Tabitha Mason!" Mr. Pearson roared. "I might expel you for your insolence. Try me again and we'll not be wasting our time with idle threats. I'll have no trouble sending you to another school without any recommendation from me."

"Point taken," Tabby barely made eye contact this time.

I felt guilty as Tabby had been defending me and I thought about coming clean and telling Mr. Pearson that we'd stolen the diary and that I was the one he should expel and send off the school grounds.

But then I looked behind Mr. Pearson at the painting of Neville. I thought of Emily and what she'd think of the two men in front of us and I decided to hold my ground.

"There's no truth to her statement then?" Mr. Pearson said.

"None whatsoever," I said as evenly as I could.

"Right, that will be all." Mr. Pearson folded his hands and turned away.

Out in the hall Hugh said, "Didn't Ms. Asquith say that Mr. Pearson had the key? So how would she have been able to check that the diary was the real one?"

"Maybe he's lost the key and doesn't want to admit it," Tabby said. "At least he didn't ask to check your bag."

"I know. If he had I'd be packing right now."

"And he would have caught you lying to his face," Tabby said. "How could you do that?"

I couldn't tell if she was impressed or horrified. I wondered if she regretted our friendship and the escapades that had followed.

I had broken every school rule except one and Tabby had been with me for all of it.

65

# The Egyptian Vault

"I think I should go it alone from here on," I said to them. "I've got you both in enough trouble already."

"We're not going anywhere, are we Hugh?" Tabby exclaimed. "He's just keeping the chair warm in there and we all know it."

"Won't he be eating his words when we find the Chagall paintings and we're all famous? You did the only thing we could have done, Mabel, kept him in the dark. He's no help to anyone at all."

# Chapter Seven

That weekend we arranged to meet at Hugh's on Saturday afternoon. *Never* in the history of my adolescent life had my parents given me permission to go over to a boy's house. But then I'd never asked before. I played up the stitches and the bullying and said I really needed some time with friends who liked me. I didn't tell them that I couldn't wait to get to Hugh's house and be outside of school with him.

Mum and Dad dropped me at Hugh's house after lunch, and I'd thought they'd both come in and meet Mrs. McGinley. But instead when we stopped, Mum put her hand on Dad's arm.

"Bernard, let's just give her a wave. Mabel can fill us in later."

I'd told them Hugh and his mum were having a hard time adjusting to living without Hugh's dad. When they pressed me for more details I had none to give.

"Be a good girl," Dad said.

Hugh lived in a white cottage with a thatched roof. It looked cosy with a pretty garden covered in frost, and smoke coming from the chimney.

Hugh opened the door and let me in.

"Mum, Mabel's here. Come and say hello."

"Be right there," she said from somewhere inside.

Tabby bounded up the path just as Hugh's mum appeared. As tall as Hugh, she had blue eyes and short wavy blonde hair. You could see Hugh's face soften when he put an arm about her shoulder to introduce us.

"Mum, these are my friends, Tabitha and Mabel."

"Pleased to meet you. Hugh's told me so much about you both. It's so nice of you to come. I've tried packing up a few boxes, but I haven't got very far. I'm still not sure whether we should be doing this at all."

"There's no doubt in my mind," Hugh said. "Now don't you worry, we're all here to help and it won't take long, you'll see."

"Thank you, darling," she said. "I know you're right, but what if he comes back and asks for his things?"

"He's not setting foot in here, Mum. Once his things are gone, we'll both feel better, and then perhaps we can start to feel normal again."

"I'm not sure I'll ever feel normal again."

"Course you will."

Tabby and I looked at each other and I wished we could step back outside. A cat mewed from the living room.

"That's Basil." Hugh showed us the living room with its brick fireplace and watercolour paintings of the sea on the walls.

"And through here is my room."

We all stood at the door. Sketches covered the walls, mostly of hands and faces, some pen and ink, some watercolour.

"Did you do all these?" Tabby asked.

"Yes, got sort of carried away."

# The Egyptian Vault

"But we've never seen any of these. I'd have thought your notebooks would be full of them," Tabby said.

"They are." Hugh went to his desk, turned on the lamp in the corner, and showed us his exercise books. All around the edges of the pages were sketches of little scenes. I wondered if he'd done the watercolour paintings in the living room so I asked him.

"I did almost all of them." He smiled for the first time since we'd come into the house.

"Hugh, you're a real talent," Tabby said. "You could go to art school and study this."

"That's what I'm planning on. Perhaps one day you'd both sit for me? It's not often I get to draw real live models."

"Of course we will." I felt impressed and a little silly that I hadn't noticed his interest in drawing before.

"I do this at home mostly." He went over to the wall beside his bed, and showed us a picture of me. I felt my face flush, and I tried not to look flustered. Tabby squeezed my hand and practically yanked it off.

"You've almost got her, except I think her hair is wider."

"Wider?" I said.

"Like Tina Turner, only shorter. She wears wigs, you know."

"It's just right." He put the sketch away in a hurry.

"Well, we should probably get to work," I said.

He showed us to his mum's room off the living room.

# The Egyptian Vault

"What exactly did you want us to help with?" Tabby asked.

"We're getting rid of all of Dad's stuff."

"Isn't that a bit drastic?" Tabby said.

"You know nothing about it." Hugh looked annoyed.

"You're right. So why don't you tell us? We want to help, don't we, Mabel? Or we wouldn't be here."

"I should have told you before. I just didn't know how."

"That's all right," I said. "You don't have to tell us. We'll help you with whatever you want."

"What I want is to make it all go away." Hugh sat down on the bed and looked around, then put his head in his hands.

"It can't be that bad, can it?" Tabby said.

"It is that bad, even worse."

We sat down on either side of him on the yellow bedspread with blue flowers. I wished Hugh didn't have to go through whatever had happened. I put my hand on his.

"You see, he had two families."

"Like an ex-wife and other children?" Tabby said.

"No, not like that."

Hugh rubbed his forehead with his hand. "Like our family and then another...both at the same time."

"Gosh, he must have been busy," Tabby said.

"He used to go to Manchester all the time to see a client, or someone we thought was a client. But we found out he'd been lying. He's great at lying. His wife and other children live there."

"So he lived a double life?" Tabby asked.

70

Hugh nodded.

"For how long?" I couldn't imagine.

"At least ten years. Mum only found out at the beginning of term. She's devastated. We both are, and he keeps calling, from Manchester of course, because he's gone to live with them. But he says he misses us and we're just devastated."

"You've got every right to be," Tabby said. "That's terrible, so selfish. How could he?"

"That's what we keep asking ourselves, so we decided to stop asking and just get rid of everything that reminds us of him. The clothes first; that's the first step for Mum anyway."

Around the wardobe door a collection of boxes stood empty. The rest of the room had professional photographs of Hugh and his mum and dad.

"Mum's a bit of a photographer, takes her camera and tripod everywhere. Never leaves the house without her case."

"Will she take those down eventually, just so she's not reminded?" I asked.

"We're not there yet. But yes, I'd like to take them down and smash them all into little pieces."

In the photos I could see that Hugh's father had dark hair, with olive skin. Hugh looked nothing like him. He had kind eyes, and a bright smile, and in every picture he looked at Hugh as if he loved him more than anything in the world.

"Has he phoned lately?" Tabby asked.

"Just this morning. Mum told him not to ring here again, to give us some space, and they ended up yelling at each other."

# The Egyptian Vault

"We'll start with the ties. They're easy, then maybe the jackets and shoes. Tabby, come and help."

We sorted the clothes into boxes and Hugh watched from the bed; then after a while he started to help. His mum came in a few times, to bring us tea, but as soon as she got close to the boxes she started to cry and then left.

Tabby asked Hugh to find some tape to close the boxes and I labelled them. Then we loaded them into the back of his mum's car. She drove us back to Lymington, to a thrift shop on the High Street. It was painfully quiet and not even Tabby said a word.

"You're good friends to help us like this," she said when she pulled over. "I'm more grateful than I can say."

"Not at all," Tabby said. "Everyone needs help sometimes."

We unloaded the boxes and then Hugh told his mum that we'd like to have something to drink and then he'd take the bus home.

"Of course, you all need to have a bit of fun, but do call if you need a lift. Don't be shy. I loved meeting you both. Hugh's so lucky to know you."

"Are you sure you'll be all right, Mum?"

"I'll be fine; now you take a bit of money." She handed it to Hugh as we got out of the car. "And don't let the girls pay for their drinks."

After she'd gone, we walked up to a restaurant on the High Street and sat down inside. We looked out and saw that right across the street from where we sat was *The Bowler's Green Auction House and Gallery*.

"Well that worked out nicely," Tabby said. "Did you bring the diary, Mabel?"

"I've got right here."

Our drinks came. I opened the diary to the bookmark and began to read:

*1910*

*Gustave has just made me the most extraordinary gift. He took me out into the garden and when we were sitting on a blanket he gave me a music box that I know I shall treasure all my days. On the top is a dancing couple surrounded by floral scrolls. When I lifted the lid, music began to play, and Gustave asked me to dance. It was almost dusk in the garden, and he held me very close and whispered that he loved me, that he would never forget me. He said they had finished their work and planned to leave the very next day.*

*I could not keep from crying and told him he could not go. He replied that he could not stay and asked me to consider coming to Paris to see him. I would love to, but how can I leave Father?*

"So where do you think the music box is now?" Tabby asked.

"Maybe she took it with her after her father died. That's what I would have done," I said.

"Or she might have left it for safekeeping in the suite until she could come back and collect it," Tabby said.

"It's worth a look," Hugh said. "You're not going to believe this."

"What?" Tabby said. "What is it?"

"Look over there, it's Mr. Reeves going into the gallery."

# The Egyptian Vault

We saw Mr. Reeves coming out of the gallery a few minutes later. For a moment he looked across the street and we weren't sure if he'd seen us, so we all ducked down in our chairs and started to giggle. Then he turned and walked back down the street.

"Funny that," Tabby said. "What do you think he was doing in there?"

"If only I could have been a fly on the wall." I started to get my things together. Then Hugh paid the bill and Tabby and I walked out onto the pavement.

"I'll walk home from here, it's not far."

"Hugh and I are off to the bus station," Tabby said. "Care to walk us over?"

After we'd said goodbye, I walked home and let myself in. It felt good to be in the flat alone. I walked up the stairs to my room and jumped onto my bed. I opened the diary again and found a sketch Emily had made of the music box. I thought about Hugh and his sketch of me. I hopped off the bed and twirled around in my room until I made myself dizzy.

# The Egyptian Vault

## Chapter Eight

Back at school the next week, we read the fifth entry of Emily's diary in the stables.

*January 27, 1910*

*Letters have been arriving from Gustave almost weekly and the latest have been the most tragic. Paris is flooding and a week ago, the waters of the Seine began to overflow in the towns upriver from Paris.*

*Gustave has abandoned his flat and has moved into an emergency shelter in a church with other homeless people. He says the river has pushed up through the sewers and that the metro lines are filled with water too. The city looks like a vast lagoon, people balancing on wooden trestles submerged in the water.*

*Gustave says that a storm led to the deluge on Paris and the entire region. Hot air balloons filled with sightseers and photographers float through the sky to view the devastation. The zoo also flooded and people say that crocodiles escaped and have been seen floating free.*

*I am terrified just thinking of it yet another part of me is eager to see the city under water, as nothing in England compares to his descriptions. Gustave has sent a photo of himself to assure me he is quite well. I have put it in the music box for safekeeping.*

*If I go to him, as he has suggested, I know the Father will disinherit me. Nellie helped me decide it would be best to go after the flood subsides, but I do not know if I can wait that long. Gustave will need to secure another flat. Perhaps his artist friends can be of some help.*

*Nellie has just brought me another letter. We have read it together, overcome with excitement. Gustave has found a flat that he needs to pay very little for. His studio will be ready in a week or two.*

*He says the flat is in a place called La Ruche, which means Beehive. It is an artists' colony in a run-down district in Paris that Gustave calls the Vaugirard. He says if I come I could stay with him, but I should know that there are slaughterhouses close by. Could I stand it? I can't be sure.*

*There are twenty-four studios in La Ruche, and Gustave says his is a large one on the top floor with plenty of light, but strangely all the studios are shaped like wedges of cheese. There is a workroom, equipped with a heater and a loft for a bed. It sounds very primitive, but together we could manage, I feel sure of it.*

*He says many of the other artists living there are Russian, Italian, German, Spanish. He has met an artist called Modigliani, and another called Lipchitz. Somehow I will find a way to see it for myself. I know now I cannot stay here with Father always gone and me dying of boredom. I must see Paris for myself, even if it costs me everything I hold dear.*

"Could the stolen paintings have come from there?" Tabby asked.

"They might have, but she's no thief." Hugh said. "If anything, I'll bet Gustave took the paintings."

"We need to go back into the suite," Tabby said.

"If we go back at night there'll be less chance of getting caught," I said. "That also means waking up at midnight."

"I'm a light sleeper," Hugh said, "always have been. I could come down and wake you both, then we could all go to the sick bay together."

+++

Tabby and I slept in our clothes that night because we didn't want Hugh to see us in our nighties. We put our dressing gowns on top so we wouldn't look suspicious if anyone came to check on us before we slipped down the hall.

When Hugh came and shook me awake, I pulled the covers back and slipped on my shoes.

"Have you got the diary, and your torch?" Tabitha got up too and adjusted her dressing gown.

We crept down the hall and silently shuffled past Edwina's room, two doors down.

"You know she's in there don't you?" Tabby said.

"Who?" I whispered.

"Edwina, of course," Tabby said.

"But she's gone; Mr. Pearson told us himself."

"And now she's back, since her father had a fit and threatened to renege on their financial commitments to the school."

If Edwina decided to follow us, then she could alert Matron and Mr. Pearson and that would be the end of everything. I hoped we'd be all right.

In the sick bay, Hugh went straight to the loose floorboard and snapped the crocodile's jaws.

Tabby and I shone our torches on the wall and as it turned we all slipped through to the other side.

# The Egyptian Vault

"Where do you think we should start, Mabel?" Hugh asked.

I couldn't imagine that Emily would have hidden the music box in the organ or behind the curtains. "I think she'd have put it in a desk."

"The library has a few desks," Tabby said. "Let's start there."

We started with the little desk in Edmond's library.

"Mabel, you didn't by any chance you bring your hairgrips with you?" Hugh said. "The drawers are locked. Do you want to try?"

"I've got two right here." The ancient locks felt stiff and well beyond my skill level. "It doesn't help that they haven't been opened for ages either."

Hugh stood above me shining the torch on my fingertips as they worked the hairgrips in the lock of the first drawer.

"I'm not sure I can manage this." I looked up at him but kept going, jiggling the grips in the lock, and then a miracle. I gave the first drawer a tug and it opened.

The desk itself had four drawers. The first looked full of papers and photographs. There was one of Emily in a pram, and one of a woman holding her. Others showed Emily walking around the grounds on very short toddler legs. In another, she held the reins of a pony. Then she was skipping with a rope on the pathway, and behind her, a huge lawn stretched out. In the middle of the lawn, a tree looked like it had fallen in a storm.

Still more of her on a swing being pushed by a very stern old lady, and then walking alone on a ridge. It looked lonely. I passed the stack to Tabby while I went through the rest of the drawer.

"There's no music box in here."

"Try the next one then. We have time," Tabby sounded reassuring.

The next two drawers had nothing to offer, just more boring papers. But we'd come this far and there was only one drawer left. When I opened it, I realized there must be something else inside hiding behind it.

"That's odd. This one's so much shorter than the others."

"Take a look inside," Tabby said.

I knelt right down beside it, on the floor, and saw something else inside - a plain strip of wood with a leather tab sticking up from it.

"I think there's another drawer back there. Hugh, could you take a look?"

Hugh crouched down beside me and slipped his hand into the hole. "I think I can just give it a tug." Seconds later, he pulled out another drawer, shorter than the others by half.

"Mabel, you look first," he said.

As soon as my hand touched the velvet pouch, I knew she must have hidden the music box inside. I couldn't imagine her father having too many velvet pouches hanging about. I pulled the strings on the top, opened the mouth of the bag and reached in. I felt a hard smooth surface about the size of my hand. When I pulled it out, I saw the two dancers that Emily had drawn in her diary.

"Open it." Tabby put a hand on my shoulder. When I opened the lid, music began to play. There were letters inside. I took the first one out of its envelope, and found inside a photograph of Gustave wearing a jacket and tie, with a V-neck sweater and long trousers. His thick, wavy hair had been cut short and he had a hand in his pocket. I thought he looked handsome.

"This envelope is from *No. 2 Passage de Dantzig*; could that be the address of the Beehive?" Hugh wondered.

"These are all from there too." Tabby looked through the rest of the envelopes. "What's that?" She peered into the music box.

I saw two gold keys on a long gold chain.

"Hold the chain up, Mabel," Hugh said.

It dangled in the torchlight and we hoped it might hold the secret to finding the paintings. As long as my middle finger, the handles on the keys had little patterns that looked like flower petals.

"What's your guess, Mabel?" Tabby asked. "What do you think they might open?"

"I've no idea. They could open anything," I replied, but I felt Emily would have hidden the stolen paintings somewhere at the bottom of the stairs off the dining room. "I think we'll have to go down those scary stairs. But that will have to wait. Matron will be up any minute now, and we all need to be in bed when she checks."

"Should we keep these things here or on the other side of the wall?" Tabby said.

"They'll never look in my things," Hugh said. "Mabel, you could take the letters. Compare them against the diary to see if there are any clues. Can you read French?"

"Not very well, but I could manage somehow."

"I could help. I'm pretty good at French."

# The Egyptian Vault

"Of course you are," Hugh and I laughed.

"What? What's so funny?" Tabby looked put out.

"Nothing. Nothing at all," we said.

We closed up the desk and put the drawers back inside. Hugh put the music box in his blazer and we went into the music room. I flipped the switch and we went through. Once we were all back in the sick bay, Hugh snapped the crocodile's jaws and we watched the wall rotate again. We went to our dormitories and got changed before we hopped into bed and pulled up the covers.

# Chapter Nine

The next day Mr. Pearson called an emergency assembly to inform us that someone had seen pupils in the halls in the middle of the night; he looked directly at the three of us. When I looked over at Edwina, she was smiling and giving us the eye too.

"I'll have you all know that this will not be tolerated. I shall personally be patrolling the halls throughout the night, and the Matrons will do their utmost to ensure this business is short-lived. If any of you think you can make a mockery of our rules, you are sorely mistaken. And if we catch, you be warned: you will be expelled."

"Unless your name is Edwina; then you're welcome to do as you like," Tabby whispered.

"Tabitha Mason, I would thank you to pay attention in assembly," Mr. Pearson glared at her.

"What'll we do now?" Tabby whispered in the hall afterwards. "How will we get back down the hall?"

"It's Edwina's word against ours," Hugh chimed in. "I think Mr. Pearson's trying to scare us."

"That's the point of the whole thing. But if they find us breaking this rule we'll be lucky to find any other school that'll take us," Tabby said.

"There is a lot to think about. But the question is how much do we want to find the paintings. I'm willing to risk it."

"That's only because you want to be a detective like your dad, Mabel," Tabby said.

# The Egyptian Vault

"No. This is more about Emily and her paintings and getting to the truth."

"I'm with you," Hugh said. "There's a very slim chance that anyone will catch us. I bet they'll only be up until midnight. They have to sleep, don't they? We'll just stuff our pillows under the covers and if we get caught, we'll say we were patrolling the halls not lurking about.

"They'll never believe that, will they?"

"It will be worth it if we find the paintings and, really, can they be up *all night*? I doubt it. I say we go tonight."

"Tonight?" Tabby said.

"The longer we wait, the more Mr. Pearson's threats will escalate," I said.

"Mabel's right. We have to go back in before the weekend and things really start to heat up."

"Well, all I know is I can't back out now," Tabby said. "I'd always regret it and wonder, what if we'd had the chance and didn't take it?"

"That's the spirit. And Hugh?"

"I'll be there in the early hours, Mabel. Don't you worry."

+++

Later that night, I couldn't get the staircase out of my mind. How would we get down the hall to the sick bay? What would we say if someone saw us? Could the staircase support the weight of the three of us? I had a feeling that's what had happened to Neville because who really just wanders off and never comes back?

So now you see why Hugh found me wide-awake. I hadn't managed to get any sleep, but Tabby had, so I gave her a gentle shake.

83

# The Egyptian Vault

"I'm no fan of this sleeping in our clothes," she whispered to me. We looked out and saw an empty hallway. "Everyone run for it!" We reached the sick bay in seconds.

I half expected someone to be sitting on one of the beds waiting for us, but there was no one. I had hairgrips, the diary, and the keys. Two torches shone back at me. Hugh went to the crocodile and snapped its jaws. Tabby and I waited by the wall for it to open.

When we crossed to the other side, something felt different, but I couldn't be sure what it was. We shone our torches around, and then went through to the staircase and ran up it as fast as we could. Once we were in the dining room, we stopped in front of the door at the back.

Part of me hoped to find the door locked, so then I wouldn't have to fall right down to the bottom of the stairs. Tabby squeezed my hand and told me to turn the doorknob. The door opened without any fuss and I walked through and stopped at the top step. I shone my torch and saw that the staircase went down at least fifty steps.

"We're right beside you, Mabel." Tabby stepped forward, looked down into the darkness, and read my mind. "Do you think anyone will know where to look for us if we fall and break our legs? Shouldn't we have told someone what we're doing? Did you tell anyone, Mabel? How about you, Hugh?"

"Not a soul," I said.

"No, no one knows," he said. "But nothing's going to happen. Let's get on before my nerves fall to bits."

# The Egyptian Vault

I started down the stairs. Once in a while I'd put my foot through a step and I'd tell the others. All the way down I held onto a thin metal railing, grimly. How did Edmond get down to the bottom? It didn't feel like a job for an old man. A lift would have been better, or a giant pulley rigged up to hold someone. When I thought of him, I held the railing even tighter, because he had been here fifty years ago, before the wood had started to rot and collapse.

I put my hand on the wall thinking a cold hard surface might reassure me but it felt cold and slimy; the rocks were dripping wet.

When we finally reached the bottom we saw only one way to go forward. The walls opened out into a kind of gallery. On one wall there were two eyeholes, at the same height. I went over and stood in front of them and when I looked out, I could see the courtyard and the stables.

I asked Tabby and Hugh to have a go. Tabby looked through the eyeholes first. "A bit strange, isn't it? It's as if Emily's dad wanted to spy on people."

"Maybe he's buried down here somewhere." The thought sent shivers down my spine; I wasn't sure I wanted to be underground with a corpse and a rickety staircase.

"So where do you think he might be?" Tabby asked.

"With the paintings, or somewhere close to them. If she went to all the trouble of hiding the paintings down here, then she'd want them to be guarded by her father. At least that's what I would have done."

# The Egyptian Vault

Opposite the wall with the eyeholes, we saw a wall with some script on it.

"Looks like an early alphabet," Tabby said.

I placed my hand on the wall, and at the end of the first line I noticed a stone that looked as if it had been set apart from the others. I pushed down and jumped back. The wall with the script on it withdrew in front of us, and another room appeared. Inside there was a mountain of rubble.

"It's a secret chamber," Hugh said. "Do you think we can get in?"

We had enough room to step over the threshold.

"I think there's something under all that rubble." I crouched down and tried to see if I could move a part of the pile. Then some of the rock shifted and we saw the hand of a skeleton.

"I think I'm going to faint, or be sick. I don't know which first," Tabby said.

I felt unnerved too but I tried to make a brave face of it. "This fellow is long gone; he's not going to hurt us. I'm guessing this is Neville and he's a long way from that fancy portrait in Mr. Pearson's office. I think he came here to find the paintings. And what's this curled up in his hand?"

"You're not going to touch it, are you?"

"Of course I am, Tabby. Then we'll know why he's under all this rubble. I'll bet I know at least one more person who'd like to know as well." I thought of Mr. Pearson and tried to imagine the look on his face when he found out what had happened to his beloved Neville.

"Tabby, you don't look well at all. Go out and get some fresh air." I noticed the smell too and felt myself gag. I put my elbow up to cover my mouth.

Very slowly, I edged the paper out of the curled fingers and for a second I wondered if the hand might reach out and grab me.

"There's a ring on that finger. Should I slip it off?" Hugh got down to examine it more closely.

"Isn't this grave-robbing?"

"It's just a ring." He slid the ring off the bones of the skeleton's barely flexed little finger.

"That wasn't so bad. Did you get the paper?"

Just as I was about to uncurl it, I felt something start to shift and rumble.

"Quick, Hugh, follow Tabby. I think the door's going to shut!" We both jumped back to the other side of the wall. Within seconds the door closed and we were on the right side of it with Tabby.

"Are you all right?" Hugh asked Tabby.

"Better now I'm not in there. What did you find?"

"This paper and Hugh found a ring."

"Do you think the paper's from the diary?" Tabby asked.

"Could be. Let's have a look. Clearly the writing looks like someone else's. I think this might have been Edmond's."

"The ring looks like the school crest." Hugh examined it closely. "Mabel, I think you're right. Neville came here looking for the paintings and this ring proves he died searching."

"Serves him right. Didn't we find out that he took possession of the school and wouldn't let Emily live here?" Tabby said.

"After she was disinherited." I felt justice had been served and I uncurled the paper. "It looks like a map. Here's the staircase and this corridor and at the end there's a big room, and another smaller room to the side of it."

"But what are these?" Tabby put her finger on some symbols. One was a bird that looked like an eagle, but it had a lion's body. "I think that's called a griffin, isn't it? This next one looks like a hawk. Maybe it's a falcon."

"What's the last one there?" Hugh asked me.

"A beetle, I think. Why do you think they're on the map?"

"It's Egyptian mythology; scarab beetles are usually blue and used in jewellery, at least in the history books I've seen."

"Maybe the symbols are a secret code. Why don't we follow the corridor?" I felt sad for Emily, and yet puzzled too. All the times Emily had said her father had deserted her, this is where he'd come to create a museum exhibit no one would ever see. Maybe he didn't need people to see it. Maybe just knowing it existed was all that mattered.

Suddenly we heard footsteps not far away. I wondered if they were looking for the paintings, or us. I felt sick to my stomach.

"Do we know another way out?" Hugh said, "I don't think I want to take off in that direction."

"There must be one, considering all the rubble that needed to be moved," Tabby said.

We went up the passageway and I looked through the eyeholes in the wall to see if the person in the tunnel had come out somewhere inside the courtyard.

"You coming, Mabel?" Hugh said. "It's going to be light soon and they'd better find us in our beds or we won't be able to come back."

# The Egyptian Vault

"Who do you think was down here with us?"

"No idea. Where's Tabby?"

"Right here. Look at these footprints."

"Couldn't those have been Hugh's on the way down? Show me your soles," I said.

"Just my trainers." He lifted his foot. The sole's treads had different markings than the ones left in the earth below and they didn't go far. We shuffled along until we reached the foot of the stairs. The person, whoever it was, might be right behind us, waiting to knock us on the head. They must have been listening to everything we'd said and maybe they'd even heard the part about finding the ring and the map. I felt done for.

As I thought of climbing the stairs I couldn't help but wonder if someone might grab onto my legs and pull me down.

"I'll go up last," Hugh said and I loved him for it.

When we got back to the suite, we stepped back into an empty sick bay. We hurried away to our dormitories before anyone could accuse us. Someone had followed us down into Edmond's tunnels and was probably still down there. Next time, I decided to make sure we had protection. I had no intention of letting my friends end up like Neville.

# The Egyptian Vault

# Chapter Ten

Next day we met to read more of the diary, hoping it would tell us how the paintings had come to Hollingsworth.

*April 11, 1910*

*I can hardly believe I have finally arrived at La Ruche in Paris. I stole away from Hollingsworth in the night, leaving only a note. I have betrayed my family and I know this is a turning point in my life. I cannot yet grasp the magnitude of what I have done, but I am led here by a feeling in my heart that I would be foolish to ignore. I am counting on that to see me through whatever trials may come. Nellie only saw me as far as the boat and when she turned to go, my courage nearly failed me, but I held Gustave's letters tight to my breast.*

*Gustave met my coach in Paris and together we walked to La Ruche. He said many women live in the artists' colony and I must try my hand at painting and modelling for him. Gustave assured me that the rents are very low. We are very close to the Vaugirard slaughterhouses and the smell is sometimes unbearable.*

*Artists from all across Europe live in these studios, and despite the smells, I am so happy to be here with Gustave!*

*We have a kerosene lamp and already the canvases cover Gustave's studio. Soup tins and eggshells litter the floor - Gustave has pushed them into a corner with a brush. I wonder how I can live like this.*

# The Egyptian Vault

*Gustave has taken me to his favourite gallery, Bernheim's, at the Place de la Madeleine, where there are canvases by Van Gogh, Gauguin, and Matisse. It is very welcoming. We often visit the Louvre too.*

*Some of the painters at La Ruche sell their work at the Market. I am encouraging Gustave to do the same. Perhaps he will be lucky and catch the eye of a gallery owner.*

"So how long do you think she'll last?" Hugh asked.

"A few months at least," Tabby said. "Then she'll probably decide that the poor life just isn't for her."

The first bell rang, signalling the end of lunch. I needed to drop some books off at the library before heading to our History of Art class. "I'll see you up there; I just need to go to the library."

Ms. Asquith must have known I'd come because I found her behind the circulation desk.

"Do you have a minute, Mabel?" She took my arm and I knew we were going to look at the case. If she asked to look in my bag then she'd find the *real* diary and that would be it.

"You know Mr. Pearson asked me to check the diary," she said, "so I came over and had a look and it all *seemed* fine to me."

I looked at her and wondered what she must be thinking, now she knew me to be a thief.

"Until I noticed the lock was undone. Do you see that, Mabel?" I nodded again. I'd been so sure I'd locked it.

"With the lock open like that, I felt obliged to check." She opened the case and then the front cover of the substitute diary.

# The Egyptian Vault

"You see, it says, *Property of Emily Hollingsworth*, right here, so there's nothing at all to worry about. That's what I told Mr. Pearson. I'm quite sure it's the real thing."

"Thank you." I wanted to know why she didn't just pick the book up and look through it. Perhaps she didn't want to know the truth because then she would have been obliged to tell Mr. Pearson, to all our peril. She stared at me a little too long and I wondered if in her own way she wanted to protect us all.

+++

That weekend I went back to Lymington. I had arranged with my dad to meet for lunch at the station. And yes, I did have an ulterior motive. I had my sights set on finding a spare pair of handcuffs in case we had to apprehend the real thief who'd been following us about under the school. If I found an extra tin of pepper spray, I thought that might come in handy too. I knew the police used it to disperse riots.

I arrived at about midday and asked if I could wait for my dad in his office. The desk clerk, Pamela, nodded. She wasn't exactly the talkative kind, and I thought that was a good thing, especially considering the true real nature of my visit.

At the station, it's all filing cabinets, telephones, and copying machines. Most of the business that goes on has to do with public disorder, vehicle crime, burglary, and people generally being rowdy and inconsiderate. I didn't expect it to be busy on a Saturday morning because the station is only open only until mid-afternoon.

# The Egyptian Vault

I took a seat and looked behind his desk at the bulletin board full of mug shots. In amongst all the faces, I noticed a poster for a suspect called Harris Walker. He had a broad forehead and thick long hair, but unlike the others, his expression suggested he'd just pulled off a job and felt pleased with himself. The mug shot seemed like a badge of honour. He was actually smiling. And in a way his smile made me think of a handsome rogue. He looked like the sort of person you couldn't help but like, someone on television, not on a board at a police station.

I didn't think he had anything to do with the paintings or the forgeries, and I can't explain why but I took his poster off the board. I saw he was wanted on charges of burglary by Interpol. That meant that police were looking for him *across Europe*. So I folded it and put it in my coat pocket.

I closed the door and shut the blinds before I went to see what might be in the drawers in Dad's desk.

I fished around, finding nothing of use and then looked in his briefcase. There I found a set of handcuffs and on the filing cabinet behind me a canister of pepper spray. I put both into my bag just as the door opened.

"Finding everything all right?" Pamela stood in the doorway.

"Oh yes, thanks." I tried to sound casual. "Is Dad on his way? It's a bit boring waiting."

"He should be down any minute now."

"Thanks."

A few minutes later Dad appeared at the door.

"Why are the blinds down?"

"They looked as if they needed a bit of dusting."

"Oh, we have people that come and do that, Mabel."

"From the looks of it, not very often."

"Right then, where shall we go for lunch?" He opened his desk drawer and pushed a few things around inside. "Can't find my keys anywhere, Mabel. I suppose we'll have to walk."

"Let's go to that new café on the corner. They've got Cornish pasties. We could share one." I knew he loved those.

"Nonsense, we'll have one each, all right?"

I looked at his tummy and he tucked his shirt in. "I've been good all week. One won't hurt."

The café was busy but we found a table in a corner where we could talk.

"So how are you doing? Mum said you had a terrible time this week."

"That doesn't begin to cover it." I showed him the stitches on my temple.

"I understand the Corrigan girl pushed you, didn't she?"

I nodded.

"They're into some trouble, Mabel. Not the kind of people we should be mixing with."

"*I'm* not mixing with *her.* She's got it in for me and Mr. Pearson suspended her then let her come back."

"I can't say I'm surprised, and I'm awfully sorry. But you are coping, aren't you? We don't need to take you out of there?"

The thought of leaving Hollingsworth, Tabitha, Hugh and the paintings made my stomach turn.

# The Egyptian Vault

"No, apart from Edwina, I really love being there. I've actually made some friends."

"I know it's been good that way, hasn't it? But I *am* a bit worried."

"Don't be. Everything is fine, it really is."

"You'd tell me if it wasn't, wouldn't you?"

"Of course I would, Dad," I replied.

"Good, because I've almost solved the forgery case. You don't happen to have had any ideas about where the paintings might be, Mabel? No, you've probably forgotten all about them, haven't you, love?" He looked up from the menu at me.

"I'm keeping my eyes and ears open. I'll let you know if I find anything out. I've just been so busy with all my prep but if I do find something out, what should I do?"

"Call right away. But keep out of trouble, please. Your mother would never forgive me should anything happen. If you even get a hint, ring me. Promise?"

"I promise."

"Be good and if you find something, please tell me. Don't think you can do it all by yourself. After all, you're only fourteen."

I wouldn't tell him until I had the paintings and could hand them over to him. That's one of my worst traits, being so stubborn, but I knew I could cope. I reached into my bag and felt for the handcuffs, spray, and the diary. Mission accomplished.

+++

On the way home, I couldn't resist stopping by *Bowler's Green Auction House and Gallery*. I went in and could hear people talking in the office so I

95

pretended to be looking at the paintings. Quickly, I made my way over to the office door, grateful that it was open. I could just make out Edwina's dad inside and another man with his back to me dressed in a tweed coat. I heard the unwrapping of paper and then Edwina's dad said, "I never would have believed you'd find them, well done."

"It wasn't the easiest thing, but when I found the crate I knew it had to have been left by Emily."

It sounded as if they were talking about Emily Hollingsworth and my heart sank as I thought someone really had got to the paintings first. That explained the footsteps in the tunnel that night.

"Have you settled the provenance issues? Because once that's taken care of, I can auction them off for a few million pounds, and then we'll be *very very* rich." Mr. Corrigan asked.

Provenance is the history of ownership of a painting and Tabby had told us that it provides legitimacy and adds value to a painting because you can't prove it easily. If the two men were talking about the Chagall paintings and intended to sell them to the highest bidder then they'd have a tricky job convincing the buyers where they'd been for the past sixty years.

"How soon before you'll be able to get the papers together?" Mr. Corrigan sounded impatient.

"I have an art historian friend who works with the *International Foundation for Art Research in New York*. They have an art theft archive. He's more than willing to help. We'll say these paintings were found in a flat in Munich, and are considered part of the art plundered during the Nazi period. If there's any question, my friend will verify our position."

# The Egyptian Vault

"Could be a tricky business, but it does sound plausible. That would strike out all the provenance issues. Yes, I think that angle will work nicely."

Then I heard a slap on the back and made a quick retreat. I waited across the street, but no one came out so I gave up and went home.

+++

The next night, I packed my bag for the week, putting the handcuffs and pepper spray in with my things. In my coat pocket I found the photo of the man wanted by Interpol. I sat on my bed and looked at him for a while, wondering why I'd brought him home. I decided to put the paper inside the bed rail for safe-keeping.

# Chapter Eleven

First thing next morning, I convinced Tabitha and Hugh to be quick about breakfast. We stopped in the dining hall for a hot cross bun and made our way to the stables. When I told them I had the handcuffs and the pepper spray they both grinned at me and shook their heads.

"We don't have much time," Tabby said when we reached the stables. "Are we going back in tonight?"

"I think tomorrow." We found a place to sit at the very back. "Mr. Pearson will be on high alert tonight. Well rested from the weekend and all."

"Mabel's right," Hugh said. "We'll throw them off a bit if we wait another day."

"Shall I start reading before we run out of time?" I took the diary from my bag and opened it.

*June 20, 1910*

*Summer in Paris has not quite been what I expected. Gustave has proposed to me repeatedly and I can't say yes. I have cold feet and I'm living with the illusion that if I don't marry Gustave I can return home and resume my life there.*

*We are poor; often I am hungry and wishing for clean clothes and my old bed. Life here is nothing like what I thought it would be, yet I have not given up hope. Some of the other artists are amusing. We continue on at the Beehive because it is the only studio we can afford. I am painting and learning French. The locals know me now, and are kinder than when I first arrived.*

*October 15, 1910*

# The Egyptian Vault

*At last I have made a friend. Her name is Bella and I met her at one of the markets. Her fiancé has recently moved to Paris from Russia, and she has come to see him. Bella says it was love at first sight when she met Moyshe Segal, her fiancé. She speaks very little French, but we both love to drink coffee in the cafes. She says her fiancé has been studying the Old Masters in the Louvre and other artists at work in the city. A senior member of the Russian parliament paid her fiancé's train fare and gives him a monthly allowance. I wish Gustave could meet such a man. We remain destitute.*

*January 15, 1911*

*At last we have met Moyshe, Bella's fiancé, who calls himself Marc Chagall. He has come to live in the studio next to ours and has become a great friend to Gustave. They have a mutual friend, a Swiss poet named Cendrars. He comes and translates Russian for us.*

*March 30, 1911*

*Yesterday, Gustave asked me again to marry him. I finally accepted! I know I cannot return to Father and I cannot live any other life but this one. We have asked Cendrars and Chagall to be the witnesses at our wedding. They have agreed. Bella will be my maid of honour. I am ecstatic. Chagall has asked if he might paint us after the wedding, as a gift.*

"Maybe she brought back those paintings," Tabby said. "Which would make them a gift to her. The police might have it all wrong."

"To think Marc Chagall witnessed her wedding," I said.

99

The bell rang and we had to go to class. We moved quickly. I closed the diary and put it into my bag. As we walked out Tabby asked me about Ms. Asquith.

"I can't believe I forgot to tell you."

"What?" Hugh said.

"I went in the other day and I think we left the case open."

"But you locked it, didn't you, Mabel?" Tabby went white.

"I can't be sure. I know at the time I felt terrified someone would catch us. All I could think about was leaving. So I don't know. But the funny thing is that when we went to the case Ms. Asquith turned to the first page of the diary and showed me Hugh's forgery of Emily's signature."

"We're all out," Tabby sighed. "I knew something would happen but I can't believe it would be something as simple as leaving the case unlocked."

"But there's more to it than that."

"So then what happened, Mabel?" Hugh asked.

"She said that Mr. Pearson had asked her to check the case and she'd told him everything was in order."

"She can't be that gullible, can she?" Tabby asked.

"I think she knows what we did and in her own way she wants us to keep going."

"So she wants us to find the paintings!" Tabby skipped along and then stopped. "But why would she care?"

"I get the feeling she's not too fond of Mr. Pearson and his rules. Maybe she's willing to make an exception for us."

"That's a pretty big exception, don't you think? She could get the sack." Tabby looked worried.

I felt guilty, again.

"Maybe she's sick and tired of watching someone get away with bullying you." Hugh put his arm on my shoulder.

"Speak of the devil," Tabby whispered.

Just as we opened the front doors I heard a voice say, "Where do you think you're going, Mabel Hartley? Don't you know that sneaking around the halls in the middle of the night will get you expelled? At least it will if I have anything to say about it."

"Leave off, Edwina," Hugh said. "Haven't you done enough?"

"Not nearly enough. Mabel's still at Hollingsworth, Hugh, and as long as she remains here, I shan't get any rest. I'll be seeing you tonight in your nightmares, Mabel."

+++

Tabby shook me awake the next morning. "Mabel, what's that all over the floor?"

"How would I know, I only just woke up." I felt as if I needed at least three hours' more sleep to feel myself again.

"It's your *hair!* Mabel, someone's come in and cut your hair off. Didn't you wake up or feel anything?"

"If I had, don't you think I'd have stopped them?" I looked at the floor. It was covered in hair cuttings. My hair cuttings. I felt my hair and there was none.

"She's done it, Mabel. She's cut off your hair in your sleep," Tabby sat down beside me on the bed.

"I'm so sorry. I should have woken up and stopped her."

I got up and went to look in the mirror, scared of what I might see. Then I started to cry and couldn't stop.

"Don't worry, Mabel," Sam said. She was small like me, but with very long shiny black hair that came almost to her waist. This was the first time she'd spoken to me. "You still look lovely to me. Did anyone see who did this?"

"We all know exactly who did this. Sam, can you go and find Matron, please?" Tabby stopped crawling around on the floor. She'd been picking up loose strands of hair and putting them in the wastepaper basket. I watched her dust off my pillow and pull the covers back to get any strands left in the bed.

"You don't have to do that, Tabby. I'm going home and I won't be coming back."

"That's exactly why she did it, Mabel, to get you to go, but you can't. We'll get you the best hairdresser and a perfect cut, you'll see."

I didn't believe her. I got back into bed and I stayed there pulling the covers up over my head. I couldn't face the day, or my school, or any of the teachers or the other pupils.

"Mabel? Go to breakfast, Tabby." I heard Matron say.

"Mabel."

I peeked my head out from under the covers.

"There, there," she put her hand on my hair. "Sit up now, it's not so bad."

"It's terrible." I fought the tears.

# The Egyptian Vault

"Nothing a first rate hairdresser couldn't fix into a lovely pixie cut. And I'll have you know I used to be a first-rate hairdresser. I still have my scissors and combs just for this kind of occasion."

I wiped the tears from my cheeks and sat up.

"I knew that would cheer you up. First things first. This is the act of a bully and I promise you if Mr. Pearson doesn't expel Edwina permanently, I will find myself another job. You have my word on that. I like you, Mabel, and I think that you're going to go a long way in life."

"I've had the most wretched hair my entire life; and there's not a thing I can do about it. I've always wanted to wear it short, but I don't have the right shaped head or face. But you're a beautiful girl, and I can make this right; will you give me the chance?"

I nodded, not trusting myself to speak.

"Come on then."

I went with her to her room across from the sick bay. After half an hour or so, my hair did look better because it looked less frizzy. I almost liked the style better; in fact, I looked pretty close to perfect.

"See," she said, "Don't you look posh? You're lucky your hair is so thick. Go and get dressed now, and off you to go class. I'll have words with Mr. Pearson immediately."

When I saw Hugh at breakfast I wanted to hide but he came straight up to me. "I heard Matron's turned her room into a barber's shop. I'll be heading straight to her after class."

I laughed out loud.

"What? She does good work. You're living proof. No more hiding your hair under that lorry driver's cap, promise?" For the first time all morning I felt genuinely happy, and my mood only further improved when Tabby told me they'd kicked Edwina out for good.

+++

Later that night, Hugh came down to round us up. I double-checked my bag for the diary, the map, the key, the handcuffs and the pepper spray.

After getting through to the suite and going down the rickety steps off the dining room, Tabby, Hugh and I followed the map and headed straight down the main corridor of the tunnel. About twenty-five feet along we heard the footsteps again. Tabby shone her torch all around us. "Do you think it's Neville, come to get us for stealing his map?"

"Hardly," Hugh said. "It's probably someone who's actually breathing."

"What if they block off the exit and we end up down here forever, turned into skeletons?" Tabby said.

The thought had crossed my mind but I pushed it out. "We're not going to be stuck, Tabby, we're going to find the paintings once and for all. I've got the pepper spray and while we're here we should try and find another way out."

"But where do you think it is?" Tabby perked up.

"Maybe the person with the footsteps knows." Hugh sounded brave. "Let's circle back and see if our intruder can show us another way out."

"Or we follow *this*." I shone my torch on the wall where an animal was painted with a bird's head and wings and a lion's body."

"That's the griffin from the map." Tabby went over and put her hand on it. "Very fine indeed."

# The Egyptian Vault

"Can anyone see any other symbols along here?" I asked.

"Here, here!" Tabby forgot about the skeletons. "There's another one a bit further down the wall here."

"If we follow the symbols, do you think we'll find the paintings?"

"Yes, I think we just might."

"But what do you make of this?" Hugh shone his torch at what looked like a beetle up on the wall.

Suddenly, Tabby's torch went out.

"Must be the batteries running low. Don't worry." I put my hand on hers. "Can you see any other symbols, Hugh?"

"Not yet, but I suspect the beetle will lead us to an exit. Let's see what else is up ahead."

A bit further along, I saw the griffin again, on the wall of the main corridor, and shortly afterwards Hugh found a falcon. We hoped the falcon had protective powers. Two tunnels branched off either side of the main corridor, neither of which had any symbols written along its walls.

We heard the footsteps again, further off, this time, but still coming toward us, and we froze.

"I don't like the feel of this at all," Tabby said.

Then I saw something strange at the top of the wall of the left-hand tunnel. In fact, two of them, one on either side of the hall, just high enough for Hugh to put his hand on.

"Why don't you reach up there, Hugh? There's something sitting in a nook on the wall."

"It's a little man, carved out of wood. Do you think this means we're close?"

"I hope so." I took it from him and rubbed it for good luck.

Slowly we walked a bit further down the tunnel. The height above our heads increased and the walls spread further apart. We walked on until we arrived at a great door carved out of stone. Like a drawbridge, at least fifteen feet high, it had a rectangular section at the top, and below that were two stone doors that looked impenetrable.

"How will we ever manage to open those?" I didn't see any keyholes and felt defeated. We'd come all this way for nothing.

"Don't give up yet, Mabel, we're so close." Hugh started looking for something, anything to get us through the door.

I shone my torch along the wall beside the great stone doors and there, built into the stone, was a tiny door. It came barely up to my waist.

"Mabel," Tabby crouched beside me. "This is it! There's a keyhole. You have to try one of the keys."

I reached for one of the keys on the chain around my neck and put it into the keyhole, feeling as if we had landed in the middle of *Alice in Wonderland*. The key turned, the door opened, and in we went in single file.

## Chapter Twelve

"That's more like it." Hugh came in behind us.

The room felt like a big caravan with a domed ceiling. The walls were covered in Egyptian hieroglyphics, column upon column of symbols, some of which we could understand, like snakes, and falcons, but there were also vases, crosses, a shepherd's staff, an altar, and a walking bird.

"It's the Egyptian' alphabet." Tabby came over and stood beside me at the wall. "Letters, symbols, but no spaces."

Beside the hieroglyphics, on a pale yellow background, there was a painting of a black jackal, seated on a platform. Beside him, two ladies dressed in white robes were clapping their hands. They had dark faces and long black hair down to their shoulders, with large shell-like earrings.

In the middle of the centre wall, we saw another painting of a man lying on a long chair that had a lion's head at the top and lion's paws at the bottom. Leaning over him was a jackal man with a long tail and human feet. Again, orange, black, yellow and white seemed to be the predominant colours.

On the end wall to our right, a falcon-headed man opened a man's mouth with a stick. There was a table between them with several vessels on it, and behind the table a fan of feathers.

"Edmond wasn't Egyptian, so why would he do all this?" Hugh said.

"It must have reminded him of all his discoveries," I ventured.

# The Egyptian Vault

"Do you think Edmond painted all these murals?" Hugh placed his hand on the wall and stood very close to it.

"He must have. I doubt very much that Gustave was down here. This would have been the ultimate secret," Tabby said.

"I still think she would have hidden the paintings here. But after what I heard at the gallery the other day, it sounds as if someone's been here already and has taken them."

"You never mentioned that you'd been at the gallery!" Tabby said.

"Oh yes, I stopped in and saw Edwina's dad talking to another man about a crate he thought Emily had left behind. They must have been talking about the Chagall paintings, and then they went on to talk about provenance matters."

"That's probably because they're forgeries," Hugh said.

"Or stolen," I added.

"Take another look at the map," Tabby said. "Maybe there's something we missed before."

I scanned it with Hugh and Tabby but nothing told us where the paintings might be.

"Look down." Hugh shone his torch on the floor.

We saw a mural surrounded by orange and green symbols that looked like altars. In the centre was a man with his arms crossed, a staff in one hand and a stick with feathers in the other. Beside him were two altars, each with a sacrificed animal, its front and back legs tied around a pole. Above the altar was a thistle. Two tall cactus-shaped plants had red and white banners flowing from them.

# The Egyptian Vault

"Come and look at this." Hugh crouched down. "There's a keyhole here too. Why don't you try your key, Mabel?"

I took out the second key and slid it into the keyhole. Again the key turned. I could see cuts in the floor shaped like a square, and a notch beside the edge of the keyhole. It seemed like the top of a vault, or something. I pulled it back and inside, I saw an urn made of white marble that made me think of Edmond's ashes.

"Can you see anything down there?" Tabby asked. "Something rolled up or perhaps a big flat case?"

"No, I can't see anything yet." I put my head down so I could look all the way inside. Then I slid in completely and on the far side spotted a flat case. I edged toward it and grabbed the handles. They were of bone, perhaps even ivory.

The case looked as if it were made of black leather. I started to feel a little dizzy, probably from lack of breath, and inched my way back, pulling the case after me.

"Help!"

"I've got you, Mabel. Hang on," Hugh pulled me back towards the opening. The floor felt rough on my skin and I tried not to complain as I skidded across it, the portfolio in my hand. Seconds later, Hugh lifted me back into the caravan room.

"Do you really think they're in there?" Hugh said.

"Of course they're in there. Quick, Mabel. Let's undo these knots and see what's inside." Tabby couldn't wait to get started.

We folded back the sides and I expected to see one or two Chagall paintings staring back at us.

Instead, the case was stuffed full of papers, dozens of them, legal documents, including Edmond's will.

"Check the seams," Tabby said. "I'm always reading about people who sew important things into the seams of a book or a bag. Here, I'll show you. Get the keys. We can use them to cut the thread."

"You're brilliant, Tabby." I handed her the keys around my neck and we all pulled at the edges of the bag.

"See, it works best if we use it like a knife," Tabby said. "There's a border here with a slight opening in it. Here's an edge that has an opening. I'll see if I can get my key into it."

We pulled the cloth back at one corner of the case, and there, beneath, could be seen a brilliant blue. We loosened the whole cloth and lifted it off the portfolio. Hugh and I put our hands on the corners and Tabby shone the torch.

"On the count of three," I said.

Underneath were two paintings, both signed *chAgAll*. The signatures were exactly the same as the ones we'd seen on his canvases at the Tate.

"I wonder if that's how he signed them before the First World War," Hugh said. "Is that part of knowing if it's a real Chagall?"

"Of course they're real Chagalls," Tabby said. "To think they've been hidden under the halls of Hollingsworth for half a century and now we've found them!"

One of the paintings was a deep saffron yellow with the Eiffel Tower in the middle. It stretched the whole length of the canvas. Lying under the tower, a bride and groom had their arms wrapped around each other. Between them, Chagall had painted a bouquet of flowers. A fiddler floated through the sky above them, riding a violet cockerel, and all around the rim of the canvas we saw different scenes: a goat with a cello, an angel hanging upside down from a tree. The tree growing up the side of the canvas had birds in it. Off in the distance, beside a small group of houses, a woman milked a blue cow.

"I'll bet you anything he painted this for them as a wedding present." Tabby's eyes shone.

The second canvas had a full moon against a sapphire sky. "This must have been the inspiration for the other painting we saw in the textbook, "*A Sapphire Moon*." I remembered the white moon rising in the sky above Notre Dame Cathedral, the bride and groom floating across the sky, and again he'd painted a white cockerel and a green goat that looked serene and bizarre at the same time. In the distance, dawn broke over a village with a painter in an orchard.

"Here they are again," Tabby said. "I don't think she stole these pictures at all. From what we've found in the diary entries, I think Chagall gave them to Emily and Gustave as wedding presents."

"When Emily left the Beehive, she must have taken them, or maybe someone saw her and *thought* she'd stolen them. That would make sense," I said.

"Especially if the person didn't know about their friendship and wanted to report her to the police."

"I feel better knowing the truth," I said.

"The groom certainly looks like Gustave," Tabby said. "They may have been his inspiration."

After a few minutes the elation started to wear off and I thought we had to get back outside so I could ring my dad and tell him we'd found the paintings.

"I think we need to move, and fast at that." I thought about the footsteps we'd heard earlier.

"Yes," Tabby said. "Let's put the case back together."

But just as we were ready to go, we heard the footsteps again. I passed the case to Tabby and told her to kneel down beside the door in the far corner with Hugh, so they were out of sight. Someone stepped over the threshold into the room.

"Mind if I join this little party?"

I saw a gun pointed at me and a black mask covering everything but the person's eyes.

"Where are the other two?"

"It's just me, this time."

"Mabel Hartley, you've proven to be quite a rival. Now where are the paintings? I know you've found them."

"No, I've only found the vault. I just looked inside and saw a case; would you help me lift it?"

"Have a look then, slowly now, and don't go getting any ideas."

"I'll need you to shine your torch in there for me." I willed him to come closer and put my hand in my bag reaching for you know what.

"No funny stuff now." He pointed the gun at my head.

"I need more light here. I can't possibly see without it." He crouched down beside the opening and leaned in. I knew if I could just get my hands on the spray I'd have the advantage.

"I think I can reach it." I pulled the canister out as fast as I could, put it up to his face and sprayed the pepper spray right into his eyes. He fell back and I had just enough time to call to Hugh and Tabby.

"Pin his arms behind his back, if you can." I tossed the handcuffs to Hugh and sprayed him again. He coughed and I grabbed his mask and pulled it off his face.

"I don't believe it," Tabby said. "You're the headmaster. How could you?"

"Where's the gun?" Hugh searched and found the gun on the floor. I felt better that one of us had it.

"Do you have anything to say for yourself?" I stood over him.

"The paintings are my birthright. My family's legacy." Tears were streaming down Mr. Pearson's face.

"They're mine too," Tabby said. "In my dreams."

"Neville's my grandfather. He came here after his brother Edmond died and he lived here with my father Caleb."

"How did you know about the paintings?" I asked.

"Did you find them?" We finally had his attention.

"Yes, as a matter of fact we did, but we won't be giving them to you, birthright, or not," Tabby said.

"But they're mine," he whinged. "Grandfather left notes that Emily had brought back some paintings from Paris. Father didn't have any interest in them and thought Grandfather had invented the whole story."

"But what about the diary? You would have known she'd brought them back from reading it," Tabby said.

"I kept some of the pages," Mr. Pearson said.

"Well, I suppose that's how you knew how to get down into the tunnels. Check his pockets, Hugh," I said.

Hugh pulled some papers out of Mr. Pearson's back pocket and unfolded them.

"These entries are from before the war. She's still in Paris. It says that Chagall left all his paintings in his studio when he went to Berlin in 1914. Gustave joined up and the regiment he was in went on a mutiny at Chemin des Dames."

"He stayed on to fight," Mr. Pearson said, "but she was a disgrace to the family. Eventually, when Gustave was shot, she came home disinherited except for a small allowance her father had left her. Grandfather inherited the estate and father came with him."

"And you came back here to find the paintings."

"You don't think I really dreamed of running a school for snotty-nosed brats, do you? I did what I had to do to find what's rightfully mine."

"How have you been getting in and out of here?" Tabby asked.

Mr. Pearson turned away.

"Show us or we'll lock you up, here in this vault and you'll have to hope we tell someone where we have left you or you'll wind up like your grandfather."

"Grandfather is down here?" Mr. Pearson's face went contorted.

"In a room back there. He got stuck with the map and now he's no more than a skeleton," Tabby said.

Hugh crouched down beside Mr. Pearson and took the skeleton's ring from his pocket. "Does this

114

look familiar? I'll bet this ring is all you'll get in the way of inheritance. I think it's better if we give it to the authorities, don't you? We'll let them know in a few months you're down here." Hugh got up and came over to me.

"Please don't leave me down here," Mr. Pearson wailed.

"Show us the way out and we shan't have to," I said.

"What do you think, Mabel? Does he deserve the same fate as his grandfather?" Hugh asked me.

I waited for a second to answer. What I really wanted was to kick Mr. Pearson in the face with my shoes on and jump on his head for a while. He'd made my life at Hollingsworth a misery but he didn't deserve to be punished by us. We been cleverer than him and we'd found the paintings. Now they would go to a good home.

"Bring him with us."

Hugh passed me the gun and lifted Mr. Pearson to his feet.

"Don't worry, I can manage him. You won't have to use it," Hugh said.

I tucked it into my bag, wondering if I ought to hang onto it for a while.

## Chapter Thirteen

We had walked almost all the way back to the stairs before Mr. Pearson showed us a small hall. It looked like a dead end, and I couldn't see a door of any kind. "There's a latch at the top," he said. "Feel along the wall where it meets the ceiling." He looked at us reproachfully.

Hugh put his hand up. "It's lying flush along the top; that's why we can't see it." He pulled the handle back and just like that a trap door folded out into the courtyard. I felt relieved we'd found a way out and wouldn't have to make a final trip up the stairs to the suite with Mr. Pearson in tow.

"How shall we get him out there?" Tabby asked. "We can't lift him, can we?"

"I'll take the handcuffs off and he can get himself out. But one false move, Sir, and Tabby will have to shoot you in the leg." I passed the gun to Tabby.

Hugh went first and after I'd taken the handcuffs off I threw them up to him so he could put them back on Mr. Pearson.

"Don't you try anything funny," Hugh said. Mr. Pearson hoisted himself up and once he was outside Hugh put the handcuffs back on him. Mr. Pearson didn't struggle. The life had drained out of him.

As soon as we were all standing in the fresh air Tabby said, "You can go, Mabel. We'll be all right waiting here with him."

I hated to leave them, but Hugh urged, "Be quick, Mabel, and find Matron. She'll help us."

116

# The Egyptian Vault

Hugh held the gun on Mr. Pearson and Tabby kept the case. I ran around to the main entrance, past Mr. Pearson's office, through the door to the staircase, and up to the Cartoon Gallery. I knocked on Matron's room across from the sick bay.

After a few minutes she came to the door. "What are you doing here, Mabel? It's not even five o'clock and you're filthy dirty."

"We've had an emergency and I need your help. I have to phone my dad."

"What, at this hour?"

"Right now. Can I use your phone?"

"Of course, come in," she said.

"I promise to tell you everything after I ring my dad, all right?"

Matron passed me the phone and I dialled his number.

"Mabel?" Dad said. His voice sounded muffled. I thought he must have sat up and switched on the light. "Have you been hurt?"

"I need you to come to the school right now. It's a bit complicated, but you have to trust me. You're going to have make an arrest."

"And who would I be arresting at five in the morning?"

"Mr. Pearson."

"You know I love a good prank, Mabel, but this is going a bit far, isn't it?"

"We've got him in handcuffs," I said slowly. "He was trying to find the paintings, but we got to them first. Then he found us and threatened me with a gun. I got the better of him though: I pepper sprayed him."

"He didn't hurt you, did he, Mabel?"

"No, I'm fine. Please come as quick as you can."

"I'll be right there. Is someone you can trust with you there?"

"Yes, Matron's here."

"I'll be right there."

After the call I explained everything to Matron as we made our way down to the courtyard.

"I never thought I'd see the day," Matron said. "This certainly is an unexpected turn of events."

A quarter of an hour later we saw the lights of the police cars coming up the drive. I ran over when I saw my mum get out, feeling so relieved she'd come too. Dad hurried over to both of us and hugged me. You could see they'd both just got up because they'd put on the nearest clothes they had at hand. Dad was wearing the old woolen coat he used when gardening and Mum her pink satin dressing gown.

"Are you all right, pet?"

"It sounds awfully dangerous, all this business, and your headmaster is in handcuffs! Dad told me you've found the paintings. Now how did you manage that?"

"You'll never believe it when I tell you." I hugged her again feeling safe at last. She kissed the top of my head. "Your father says you're going to be a first rate police officer one day. It's all he can talk about."

Dad's eyes brimmed with tears.

"Thanks for coming," I whispered. "Now, can I show you the paintings?"

"Right after we get Mr. Pearson into the back of the police car," Dad went over to Hugh and took the gun away from him.

# The Egyptian Vault

"If you don't mind, I'd like to see the paintings too," Mr. Pearson said, a hint of hope in his voice.

"You'll be seeing them in the papers, Sir. Now get him into the back of the car before I do something I might regret," Dad said to the two policemen who'd accompanied him.

Once they'd locked Mr. Pearson in the back Dad asked to see the portfolio.

"Chagall's signature right at the bottom. Can you see that, love?" he said to my mum. "They certainly look like the real thing to me."

"To me too," Mum said. "Well done, Mabel. I'm still not sure how you managed it."

"Tabby and Hugh came with me the whole way, and we haven't even shown you the tunnels yet. And, Matron, you have to see the secret suite that's behind the sick bay wall."

"All in good time," she said. "What's most important is that you're all safe. In the meantime, I could use a cup of tea. How about I make some for all of us?"

Later, after the sun had risen, we went back through the trap door and took a look at the tunnel. I even showed Mum and Dad Neville's final resting place. Mum fainted and we revived her outside. Tabby waited with her while we showed my dad the vault.

+++

Next day at lunch everyone gathered in the courtyard to go down to have a look in the tunnels, especially after a forensics team had come and removed Neville's remains. For a few days afterwards, everyone, including the newspapers, seemed desperate to talk to us. My mum even started a scrapbook for press clippings.

Dad came to the school later in the week, but he didn't stop to talk to us so I knew he had to be on official police business there on the school grounds. When he came out he had Mr. Reeves in handcuffs.

Afterwards he came to talk to us.

"What's Mr. Reeves involved in?" Hugh asked him. "Or can you even tell us?"

"He's been tied up with Mr. Corrigan at the *Bowler's Green Auction House and Gallery*. The apple doesn't fall far from the tree where Edwina is concerned."

"It all makes sense now," I said. "He was the one in the gallery talking to Edwina's father about questions of provenance for these paintings, but I thought he'd found Emily's paintings first."

"I don't think he ever set eyes on the genuine paintings. They'd devised a scheme to fool the highest bidders. Mr. Reeves made expert forgeries and even fooled Mr. Corrigan into believing he had the genuine article."

"So you're going to charge Mr. Corrigan as well?" I asked.

"I expect so. We'll have to see how deep his connections are with criminal circles. But once this gets out everyone will know he's attempted to sell stolen paintings for millions of pounds. Conspiracy charges are certain to follow for both men and they could go to prison for years."

I thought about Edwina and despite everything I felt sorry for her. No one deserved to have a criminal for a father.

# The Egyptian Vault

"I would never have thought Mr. Reeves had it in him to peddle fakes," Hugh said.

"He had the skill to produce them," Tabby said. "We saw that in class. But who'd have ever thought he'd be involved in something criminal?"

"There's something else about Emily that I wanted to tell you," my dad said.

"What is it?" I asked.

"It seems she had a child with her when she returned from Paris. Gustave died in battle and she came to hide the paintings here, where she thought they'd be safe from her unscrupulous relatives. Then she moved to London and opened a gallery to promote European artists."

"How do you know all this?" I said.

"Someone came to me, someone you know quite well, I'm told."

"Who might that be?" I asked.

"Ms. Asquith, the librarian. Apparently, she's Emily's granddaughter."

"She's the rightful heir to the paintings then," Hugh said. "What is she going to do with them?"

"Nothing yet. We're still working on the authentication process, but she's said she'd like to have them put on exhibition. At the Tate, and they've agreed to take them. One more thing," he added.

"I've contacted the French police about the paintings. They told me that after Chagall left Paris for Berlin in 1914, all his canvasses from La Ruche went missing and some even turned up on the roof of a rabbit hutch. Someone must have slipped them off to Emily, so there she was, leaving with two. They assumed she'd stolen them."

# The Egyptian Vault

"But she didn't, Dad," I said. "He gave her the paintings as gifts. They were hers to take."

"I know. It's a remarkable story isn't it?"

"So what's going to happen to Mr. Pearson and Mr. Reeves?" I asked.

"Charges are pending for both of them and that's all I know for now. But with your testimony, they'll be going to prison for a good long time."

+++

Six weeks later, we went to London, to a special room in the Tate Gallery where there was going to be an unveiling ceremony. We took our seats in front of two paintings on gold stands covered with black cloths. Between them at the front stood a podium.

"The curator's going to speak first," Dad said.

A moment later a fair-haired man, with a very slender build and lots of freckles, stepped onto the podium. By now, loads of news-people had gathered with cameras and microphones and Dad said the press wanted to talk to us afterwards about how the paintings had been recovered.

"My name is Benjamin Fletcher and I have the very distinct honour of presenting two paintings by Marc Chagall that have been recovered by three very courageous fourteen-year-olds. The works had been brought by Emily Hollingsworth from Paris to her father's estate in Milford on Sea. We have evidence from the artist that the paintings are authentic and that he gave them as a wedding gift to Emily and her husband before the First World War."

"Miss Mabel Hartley, Miss Tabitha Mason, and Master Hugh McGinley recovered the paintings, which Emily had hidden on the estate and now I should like to present all three of them with letters of thanks from the Gallery. Perhaps Mabel, Tabitha and Hugh could come forward and help us unveil the paintings."

We all rose to applause and turned to face the crowd. Tabby and I pulled the sheet off *Emily and Gustave 1911*. Hugh pulled the cover off *A Sapphire Moon 1911*. Everyone clapped again and then the questions started.

"When are you going to start working for your father?" a woman from the *Times* asked me.

"I'm actually being recruited by MI5, but he doesn't know that yet." Everyone laughed except Dad.

"How did you find the paintings?" another asked.

"With a lot of luck," Tabby said.

We told reporters how we found the secret suite, the tunnel beneath the school, and the vault with the paintings. The photographers wanted a picture of the three of us. While they snapped their photos, I saw Ms. Asquith and another woman slip into the room and take seats very close to the back. Ms. Asquith wore a lovely suede suit with a fine pair of high-heeled shoes and she looked very pretty.

"It's her," Tabby said. "I didn't think she'd come."

"I didn't think she'd miss it," Hugh said.

"We should go and talk to her, don't you think?" Tabby said once the cameras had stopped.

"I came to congratulate you all," she said. "I've wondered about these paintings for years, and I had almost given up hope of ever finding them, but then you three showed up and the rest now is history. I knew you'd clear Emily's name – she deserved that much at least."

"Is Emily still alive?" Tabby asked.

"No: she passed away many years ago but I know she would have loved to have seen the paintings like this. And how brave you've all been."

"But why didn't she come and get the paintings herself during summer holidays or something?" Hugh asked.

"I think she wanted to put all that behind her. She never got over losing Gustave and then being disinherited by her father and uncle."

"Didn't Emily ever tell you where the paintings were? I mean you could have gone and got them for her," Hugh said.

"I could have, but she never talked about them, or what had happened at La Ruche, or even that she had met Marc Chagall. It was the happiest time of her life. She told my mother she'd never talk about it again, perhaps because, with the paintings hidden, she was keeping a little part of the past safe from the clutches of modern men like Mr. Pearson."

"Where's your mother now?" I felt anxious to meet Emily and Gustave's daughter.

"Right here," Ms. Asquith said. "She's come to see for herself. I couldn't keep her away."

Ms. Asquith waved to a very elegant woman standing off to one side of the gallery and beckoned to her to come over. She smiled and hesitated for a moment before joining us.

"Maman, this is Tabby, Hugh and Mabel, the schoolgirls and schoolboy I've told you so much about."

# The Egyptian Vault

"A pleasure to meet you," I said.

"I'm Bella Asquith. I'm so pleased to be here with you."

"Bella runs the gallery that Emily founded; she's named after Chagall's wife," Ms. Asquith said.

"Where is the gallery? I'd love to see it," I said.

"In Covent Garden. It's been running for fifty years." She paused before adding, "I'd like to take a closer look at the paintings for myself. Thank you so much for all you've done."

"I'll be with you in a minute, Maman," Ms. Asquith watched Bella walk over to the paintings.

"What do you think about Mr. Pearson and Mr. Reeves being arrested?" Tabby asked Ms. Asquith.

"Not a moment too soon. I always had a funny feeling about both of them. They weren't at the school for the right reasons, but I couldn't say a word. I'm just a librarian after all."

"What will you do now?" I asked. "Will you stay at Hollingsworth?"

"Hollingsworth hasn't seen the last of me. But I might go into the gallery business myself. I think I stayed there because I thought I might be able to help someone find the paintings, and in my own way, I think I did that."

"I don't think we ever thanked you for concealing our tracks, you know, when we swapped the diary. If Mr. Pearson had found out what we'd done, we would have been proper done for," I said.

"I felt happy knowing you had a chance. No need to say thank you. Now I think I'll go and join my mother." Ms. Asquith said. "Please do stay in touch. I'd love to hear all about your adventures. I don't think this is last I'll hear of you three."

# The Egyptian Vault

"What now, Mabel Hartley?" Hugh said after she'd gone.

"I saw a newspaper article about some Bronze Age Treasure that's been discovered in Scotland."

"And?"

"I'd like to see if we could find some ourselves."

Tabby put her arm around me. "I'll only come if you promise to find a way for us to go without our parents."

"Would you like to come too?" I asked Hugh.

Hugh didn't look so sure. "Mabel, I'll come on one condition."

"What's that?" I felt like my heart might skip a dozen beats.

"You must promise to model for me so I can make a proper likeness of you."

"But what am I supposed to do with you two fawning all over each other?" Now Tabby looked as if she needed convincing.

Hugh and I blushed.

I wondered how I'd ever persuade my parents to let me out of their sight for a whole summer but I knew I had to think of a way.

I still had some questions of my own to resolve that I hadn't told anyone about. The picture of the thief Harris Walker wouldn't let me be and I wondered why I felt so compelled to take him out of my bedpost and look at him. I hoped if I could get into my dad's office and do a few searches on his computer I might find some answers.

Leaving the Tate, Hugh swooped me into his arms and we ran down the stairs with Tabby. Summer time couldn't come soon enough.

# The Burial Chamber
# Excerpt from Book 2

## Chapter One

I've been wishing for a holiday without my parents for as long as I can remember and now it's actually happening. We're on our way to Inverness, and the best part is that we get to take the sleeper train, which means no one will be telling us what to do from here on.

I'm travelling with my friends Tabitha Mason and Hugh McGinley and we're all stunned that our parents actually agreed to let us make the journey alone, but we are fifteen now so maybe they've decided to give us a little bit more slack.

My dad pulled me aside that morning. I knew he couldn't resist at least *one* more lecture.

"Now, Mabel." Dad lowered his voice so the others wouldn't hear. "I know you're getting more grown-up all the time, but I want you to promise me that you won't go looking for any trouble. Are you listening, Mabel?"

"Yes, I'm listening, Dad." But I had no intention of promising anything of the kind, at least not without my fingers crossed behind my back. "We'll be good, won't we?" I'd looked over at Tabby and Hugh.

"Very much so." Tabby looked more innocent than a child at a church picnic. That was part of

1

being an actress, which is the one and only thing Tabby wants to be when she grows up.

The three of us met last year at Hollingsworth School, which is near our home in Lymington, and we've been best friends ever since. Tabby and I are sharing a berth and there's a little ladder between our beds that folds down from the wall. It feels as if we're being whisked away to another place and time (which in fact we are). Hugh's sleeping in his own compartment across the corridor.

"I still can't believe we're away." Tabby beamed at me.

We were sitting on plush red velvet seats, waiting for dinner to come. The compartment smelt a bit musty. Hugh got up and opened the small window above our heads.

"That's more like it." He took off his jumper and tossed it up onto the luggage rack with his suitcase. He had a new haircut, very short on the sides with a mop of curls on the top. When he rolled his sleeves up, I could see Hugh had been rowing a lot to pass the time.

"I'm roasting. How can you girls be comfortable when it's so hot in here?"

I didn't mind watching Hugh. We'd been out of school for a few weeks and I'd missed them both.

"That's better." He sat down opposite us. "Fill me in on the latest news."

"We celebrated my mum's birthday this weekend, and it was all I could do to keep my nose out of the extra tin of icing in the fridge. So I brought it with me." Tabby dug around in her gear beneath the seat and produced a tin of whipped vanilla icing and a few spoons.

2

# The Burial Chamber

"Usually I carry a Swiss Army knife, but it never hurts to have a couple of spoons for back up." She opened the lid, stuck her spoon down into the icing and brought out an enormous scoop.

"How's your mum anyway? The last we heard she was hiding out at home." Hugh took one of Tabby's spoons and started on the icing too.

"She's terrible. They call it agoraphobia. She never gets out, won't let anyone in, and she just can't sleep. I'm so glad to be away from it all."

Tabby has red hair, which she wears pinned up in a clip off her forehead because someone at the department store perfume counter told her she had the most beautiful eyes and ought to show them off.

"You're looking very slim, Tabby." I wondered how she'd managed that.

"I've lost two stone." She pushed her hand down over her front, smoothing out her sweater. "I stepped up the karate training to keep my mind off it all. Dad's been home to look after Mum. They might get a nurse."

"I'll bet that costs a lot," Hugh said.

"Dad will do anything for my mum."

"And how have things been for you, Hugh?" I asked.

Night closed in and the cabin felt darker. We'd left London at nine in the evening and the journey to Inverness takes at least eleven hours. We'd wake up there in the morning.

"Terrible. Awful. I wish my mum had something that kept her at home or she wouldn't have this new boyfriend who's old enough to be my brother." Hugh licked the end of the spoon and then gave it a wipe with his hanky. "I can't stand seeing them

3

together; he's short and smarmy and calls her "babe", and she giggles."

"How come they know each other?" I asked.

"They met at the Help Centre. It gets people back on their feet and in special cases, I suppose, they get a new boyfriend to start over with."

"Don't be too hard on her. She did find out that your father had another family just last year. It probably makes her feel better having someone around who likes her." I felt bad for them both.

"She definitely likes that part. I just don't trust him. I think he's after the house."

"He won't get it. She's much too clever for that."

Hugh looked worried. "I suppose you're right. I think I'm just annoyed with both my parents for different reasons now. I want a *normal* family, like yours, Mabel."

"You want a mother who goes away on planes and never comes home and a father who lives just so he can make the next arrest?"

"She comes home but it's never when you're there. Did something happen between you two?" Tabby put down the teen magazine she'd been skimming through. She loves to collect trivia because she thinks it will make her a better actress. She says teen magazines help her stay relevant, but I know she just likes to look at the boys in them.

"Nothing happened. Mum wanted a job with the airlines and she got it. It's just that her job's more important to her than I am. That's why I asked about finding something for us to do this summer. I wanted to get out of the house, especially after seeing that article on Bronze Age treasures in Scotland."

4

# The Burial Chamber

"We all wanted to get out of the house," Tabby said.

Hugh dozed off and I picked up the paper he'd been reading. He could always sleep, anytime, anywhere especially if there was some sort of an engine running. After a few pages, I stumbled on another article, this one about Bronze Age discs.

"Tabby." I tapped her gently with my foot.

"What is it?"

"This article says they've found treasure in the Outer Hebrides. Where's that?"

"It's a group of islands off the West Coast of Scotland. Pretty far north I think. What's the date of the article?"

"Today, the third of July, 1981."

"Hugh." I nudged him awake. "This article says they've found some Bronze Age discs from 700 BC. That's 2600 years ago. Imagine that."

He didn't look nearly as interested as I'd hoped. "Has dinner come yet?"

"There's someone at the door. Let them in, would you, Tabby?"

"Perfect timing." Hugh stretched his legs and I marvelled at how strong he looked. Over the year we'd known each other, he'd changed from a boy into a young man, filling out in all the right places, but I liked his smile best of all.

"The conductor's here with what looks like shepherd's pie. Can I pass one to you, Hugh?" I asked.

Hugh nodded and brushed the sleep from his eyes. "When did I nod off?"

"Only about half an hour ago." I put the tray on his lap.

"Smells better than I thought it would."

We all sat and ate in relative quiet. I wondered if anyone had a radio we could tune in to.

"I've got my Walkman if anyone wants to share the headphones with me." Tabby pulled it out of her pack.

"What's on it?" I asked.

"Blondie, and ABBA are on one side and U2 and Duran Duran on the other. My brother Barnaby made it for me as a going away present."

"So your brothers aren't all bad, are they? I'll listen with you." I moved over to the other side of the compartment and we all finished our dinner and then put the trays on the floor.

Hugh dozed off again and I listened to Blondie sing *Call Me*. I wondered if Hugh and I would ever be more than friends.

"So, did he call?" Tabby whispered.

"Who?"

"You know who."

"No, not until I phoned to tell him Mum had found someone who'd take us for the summer in Scotland. I haven't seen him at all."

"Is that good?"

"No, but I'm glad he's here now."

Tabby gave me a nudge and pointed in Hugh's direction. He was smiling even though he kept his eyes closed.

"I'll just go and brush my teeth." I felt embarrassed.

When I came back, Hugh had gone to his own compartment across the corridor. It took me a moment to pull the bunk down from the wall, and change into my pyjamas, which I've cut the labels out of because they say size 12.

I'm trapped in the body of a ten-year-old-boy with very short curly blond hair, but the good thing is that I can wriggle in and out of all sorts of places most people couldn't think of getting into. The other *vital* thing you should know about me is that I hate my name and not in your usual, every day way either.

My parents named me after someone, and by the way they look when they say her name I imagine she used to help children out of burning buildings. But when I ask them about her, they won't let on. All I know is I'm stuck with being Mabel Hartley, and no one likes my name except my mum and dad, and of course burning-building Mabel *must* have liked her name too, because she was a decorated hero, at least in their minds.

"Night, Hugh." I called after I'd climbed in to my bunk and crawled under the covers.

Dressed in pyjamas and a dressing gown, he walked over to my bunk, smoothed my hair with his hand on my forehead and then kissed me very lightly on the lips. I closed my eyes and prayed Tabby wouldn't walk in.

"Goodnight, Mabel. I've missed you, you know." He even smelled good. I wanted to get closer.

"You need a *Do Not Disturb* sign on the door, *obviously!*" Tabby had a mud mask on her face and looked very funny.

"Sorry, Tabby. I'll get out of your way." Hugh winked at me and touched my nose gently with his finger. Then he made his way back to his berth.

"So?" Tabby asked after she'd washed her face.

7

I didn't answer her.

"I'm not stark raving mad, you know? He kissed you, didn't he?"

"Spy much?"

"No, but I could tell when I came in that I'd interrupted something *very* important."

I giggled, feeling delighted.

"So I was right, he did kiss you. I *knew* it!" She jumped up from her bunk and crawled up to where I was lying.

"Give me some blankets, would you? And details! I want to hear everything."

I felt powerless to resist. "He came up, leaned in and kissed me. I closed my eyes. Isn't that what you're supposed to do for your first kiss?"

"Sounds like a dream. I've never been kissed, you know."

"I know, but maybe this summer you'll meet a handsome redhead and you'll have red-headed children and talk about this being the summer you fell in love."

"It's a bit early for that, don't you think? We're only fifteen. I don't plan on falling in love for at least another five years."

"I expect you'll fall in love a bit sooner than that. You know we're going to have the best summer ever! I can feel it. Now maybe you ought to go back to your own bed before I push you out onto the floor."

"You wouldn't."

"I might."

+++

When we woke the next morning, we folded our bunks up against the wall and got dressed and

8

# The Burial Chamber

waited for breakfast. When it came, Hugh passed the first tray to me. I could feel his leg touching mine on the seat and I didn't dare move it.

"It's sausage, bacon, and eggs with toast and jam. All my favourites." Tabby picked up her knife and fork.

"Has anyone looked outside yet?" I asked.

Tabby raised the window blind and we saw a barren landscape with craggy hills, very few trees, a bit of open morning sky and grassy valleys. We passed some lakes, which the Scots call lochs. It looked quiet and windswept, but desolate too.

"So, where do you want to go when we get there?" I asked.

"Straight to Loch Ness; I *have* to see the monster. I'm sure Nessie will come up if I'm there."

"Oh, you can't be serious," Hugh said.

"I'm deadly serious. It's part of the reason I agreed to come. I'll never get a chance like this again."

"And you, Hugh, what do you want to do while we're in Scotland?"

"I'd like to do some hiking and explore Inverness and get out a bit."

That sounded *so* boring, but I'd go along if it meant being with Hugh.

"Did you want to tell us about the parcel, too?" Tabby said.

"Not yet."

"Come on, out with it." Hugh nudged me.

"All I can say is there might be some night vision goggles, some binoculars and a camera on their way to Inverness. I think they're military cast-offs but the shop in Knightsbridge told me they work perfectly well."

"Why you waste your money on stuff like this I'll never know," Tabby said.

"You sound just like my dad. Last time the pepper spray and handcuffs saved the day. We'll need these things for any possible eventuality."

"Don't discourage a great mind at work, Tabby. Mabel's right, the pepper spray and the handcuffs did save the day."

Hugh put his tray aside and rummaged through his bag.

"What are you doing now, Hugh?" Tabby asked.

"Just sketching."

"Not Mabel, *again*?"

"No, the compartment. I thought if I could put a few sketches together of our trip to the Highlands of Scotland, then maybe they could go in my art school portfolio. You can't have too many pieces to choose from."

"So that's what you're set on?" I asked.

"Now more than ever. It's what I want, especially after spending so much time in the galleries last year. I'd love to see my work in a museum or just about anywhere."

"You sound like you've got great hopes." I felt happy for him.

"So did you ask your mum about the lady we're staying with?" Tabby always wanted to know more.

"I know that she's rich, and that her health is a bit dodgy. We need to keep an eye on her: she has asthma and fainting spells."

"Oh, great! Sounds like she's ninety and needs a nurse." Tabby wiped her mouth with her napkin. "I

10

don't fancy being a nurse to anyone. I came here to get away from all that."

"I'm sure she'll be fine." I hoped I was right.

"What about the house?" Hugh asked.

"It's old and bigger than Tabby's house, I think." I passed them a leaflet my parents had given me. We saw pictures of tennis courts, a meadow, a view looking out over Loch Ness. The house looked very old and posh, somewhere a lord and lady might live.

It's nothing my family had ever seen the likes of, but Tabby's family could probably afford to live there. They go on lots of holidays. They even have ponies, but Tabby prefers karate to horse riding. She's a bit of a tomboy, just like me. In a family full of brothers, Tabby came last but she's the best of them all.

+++

An hour later we pulled into Inverness station. We saw seven platforms and an information board on the far wall, with all the departure and arrival times.

"Do you know what this Rose lady looks like?" Tabby asked.

We walked out to the concourse where I half expected bagpipes to be playing and Highland games. Instead, we saw pay phones, a bookshop, a ticket office, as well as a hairdresser's and a café. It didn't look like a bad place to wait.

"I think she's right there, waving at us." I picked up my bag. "Let's go. We want to make a good impression." We walked over and shook hands.

"You must be Rose. I'm Mabel Hartley and this is Tabitha Mason and Hugh McGinley."

# The Burial Chamber

"Welcome to Scotland!" She had a charming accent. She looked middle-aged with short blond hair and a thin face. I had expected her to be old and frail with blotchy skin, but she wore clogs and a pretty floral dress with a red cardigan.

"My mum told me the woman who owns the house is an archaeologist."

"Yes, for years she used to travel to various dig sites. We didn't get along very well."

"I'm sorry to hear that."

"I hear it's not uncommon with sisters. Now that she's gone, though, I miss her."

"I'm so sorry. Mum never said a word about that."

"No, I didn't tell her. I thought she might shy away from sending ye and I so wanted to meet ye. Everyone must want to meet ye, considering those treasures ye found at your school."

"Not everyone," Tabby chirped from the back of the car. "We haven't heard from the Queen, and I felt sure she'd call and invite us to Buckingham Palace." As we crossed the bridge over the river, Tabby stuck her head out of the window. "Look, I can see Nessie's tail."

I looked but I couldn't see a thing.

"Made you look," Tabby laughed.

Rose pointed out of the window. "The house is over there up on the hillside among the trees. Can ye see it?"

I saw a stone building set apart from the city, standing out against the green of the hillside.

"The estate originally belonged to a Templar knight who fled to Scotland from the Middle East after one of the Crusades. At that time, Scotland accepted the knights when no one else would. Our great-grandfather, who started an iron foundry, drew up plans for the house as it stands today, and began building it in 1726. While I think of it, don't let me forget to tell ye about the peat bog at the back of the estate. It's a bit of a hazard."

"Why?" I knew something about peat bogs.

"Because it's not the sort of place ye'd want to get stuck in. Ye could be found a few thousand years from now all brown and leathery. I haven't scared ye, have I?"

"It takes quite a bit to scare Mabel." Hugh reached over and gave my shoulder a squeeze.

## Chapter Two

Rose drove along some country roads and it felt like a world away from home. We crossed a bridge where the trees bent very low over the car and everything looked lush and old. We looked down at a gorge beneath us. I half expected to see fly-fishermen casting their rods into the rocky stream. We turned onto a very secluded road and after five minutes I wondered how much further the house could be.

"Now it's probably best to get the house rules out of the way first." Rose drummed her thumbs on the top of the steering wheel and turned down the radio. "Your mother says ye're quite an independent lot; that said, I want to see ye every morning for breakfast and every evening for dinner. Ye're not to be in each other's rooms at night either. She said ye're all just good friends, but you never know what can happen during a summer in Scotland."

She winked at me.

"Obviously, that rule's not for me." Tabby adjusted her shorts.

"I should also let ye know that my health is good, but I have had a few fainting spells. Nothing serious yet, but I'm most grateful for your company. As it can be quite lonely at times. I thought I might like to share the house with some young people. Please don't make me regret my decision."

Seconds later, we came down a great drive. I know we'd seen photos, but nothing could have prepared us for the three-storey, grey stone mansion with carriage houses on either side. Four gabled round towers, two on either side of the front entrance, complemented the façade.

Rose got out and led us inside.

"This is the entrance hall. Quite something, isn't it?"

"It's amazing." Tabby looked up. "You really live here?"

"I have all my life. Ye'll get used to it. D'ye see the upper gallery around all three sides?"

We saw a mahogany clock case built into the railing and a row of small posts lined up and held together with a big banister. I imagined fine ladies once standing there, listening to conversations from below. All around the ceiling, leaves, birds and fruit had been carved into white plaster. Beneath our feet, black and white squares looked like a chessboard.

"What's this?" Hugh stopped in front of a black panel about three feet wide and three feet tall, next to the front door.

"That's the bell board. It works like an intercom between all the rooms. Mother had the board installed in 1913. Some things do last. Ye press the button for the right room and speak into this." She pointed to a black cone with a white rim. "A bell chimes before your voice comes through."

Hugh looked at me and I hoped we'd be having many midnight conversations. Most of the rooms had funny names.

"You'll be in Miss. Dundas's room."

"Who was she?" Tabby asked.

"One of mother's great-aunts. Hugh, I've put you across the hall, in Sir Walter Scott's bedroom."

15

# The Burial Chamber

We poked about for a few minutes and Rose showed us where we could hang our coats and leave our shoes. I walked around the bottom of a great staircase and looked at a table that had some books on it, *Bronze Age Treasures of Western Europe* and *Bodies of the Danish Bogs*. I noticed that both of them had been written by a woman named Gertrude Blythe.

I flipped through them and found a photo of a ghoulish young girl's skeleton with frayed hair, a gaping mouth, and skin stretched taut against her skull. The caption said she had been discovered in an oak coffin. I closed the book and thought I'd come back to her later.

"These books are marvellous. Do you have any more we could look at?"

"They're my sister's books. She wrote dozens of them. These two I liked best. The others I didn't care for much."

"Can I ring my mum, please?" Hugh asked.

"Go down the hall to the red drawing room. Ye'll find the phone in there. Try not to be too long as we have to pay for each call."

The three of us walked down the hall and entered an ornate sitting room with a white marble fire surround. Papered with red damask, the walls had portraits that made the subjects look thirty feet high. It reminded me of a museum. We soon found the rotary dial phone.

"We could have a parade in here, it's so huge." Tabby flopped into one of the chairs.

Hugh dialled his mother and stood for a moment waiting.

# The Burial Chamber

"Mum?" He wrapped the red cord around his finger. "We've arrived. Just wanted to let you know we're safe and sound. Rose seems very nice. How are things with you?"

"Oh, you're off to a dance with David tonight?"

He didn't say anything for quite a while.

"I am trying to be happy for you, Mum."

He put the phone back on the receiver.

"Is she all right?" Tabby asked.

"Yes, she's fine. She couldn't be happier. I feel like the worst son in the world."

"Nonsense, it's good you called, and now you can forget about them, can't you?" Tabby said.

"It's not that simple. I worry that she might get hurt. He's too young for her. She should know better. I'd be surprised if he's twenty. But there's not a thing I can do about it."

"We should call home too, shouldn't we?" I picked up the phone.

We both rang home, but no one answered. A few seconds later, we heard a shriek and we all dashed back the way we'd come.

"Rose, can you hear us?" Tabby shouted.

"In here."

"I think she's this way." Hugh passed the staircase and went down the hall to the room beyond it. "Come on, she's in the kitchen."

At the far end of the room was a great hearth, with cream-painted cupboards and a red lino floor. In the middle of the room was a large pine table that looked as if it could seat twenty people, and over by the sink was a butcher's block table with vegetables scattered over it.

"I must have slipped."

Tabby got down on her hands and knees. "She's behind the island in front of the stove."

"Rose, are you all right?" I got to her first. "What happened?"

She was lying on the floor with her eyes closed and a bit of blood was trickling down her forehead. Her pulse was racing. Checking it was the only medical thing I knew how to do. I propped her head on my lap and her eyes fluttered open.

"Not exactly the best start to a holiday, is it? My puffer's in my bag on the counter over there. Would one of ye bring it over to me, please?"

Hugh looked about. "Your puffer?"

"For my asthma. It's an inhaler, in the front pocket of my bag." She wheezed and gripped her chest.

Hugh raced over to her green satchel bag on the counter by the sink. He found the inhaler and brought it over to her. She took a deep breath, sucking the medicine into her lungs, and repeated it twice more.

"Dreadful way to have ye start your holiday. I'm so sorry." Her colour came back and she sat up ever so slowly.

"These things happen." I smoothed her hair. "Whatever caused this?"

"It's my asthma acting up. When I slipped on the wet floor I had the wind knocked out of me. Now that I feel quite well again, would ye check the kettle and make me some tea? Not too strong, please."

Tabby went over to the sink and ran some water on the cloth that hung on the tap. Then she filled the kettle and put it on.

# The Burial Chamber

"I must have hit my head against the side of the island when I fell. This is all very awkward. I'd meant to take ye on a lovely stroll around the garden."

"There's lots of time for that. Let's help you up." Tabby passed me the cloth and I gave it to Rose. We led her over to a window seat that looked out on a rose garden. Beyond it, we could see the water.

Tabby looked out. "Is that Loch Ness?"

"The very one, and ye'll be able to see it from your windows upstairs."

"Have you ever seen the monster?" Tabby asked.

"Not since I was a child."

"What did you see?" Tabby looked thrilled.

"I've seen the humps several times, coming to the surface of the loch, usually on days that are dark and grey. I can see them from up here. I've a telescope outside, ye see."

"Might I go and have a look?" Tabby asked.

"By all means, there's a boy about your age who lives down the road. He's always riding up wanting to look through the telescope too."

"What's his name?"

"Tom. I expect he'll be round to see ye sometime soon. I told him ye were coming. I think ye'll find him pleasant company."

Tabby stepped outside and peered through the telescope, then waved for me to come out too. The loch looked calm and on the far side, cloud cover hid the mountains.

"I can't see any boys through this, or the Loch Ness monster for that matter."

"We'll keep our eyes peeled. Let's go back in and get settled down."

"Do you feel well enough for us to go and find our rooms?" I asked Rose.

"Of course, ye'll want to get settled in, won't ye? Ye turn right at the top of the stairs and go down the hall. Ye'll find your rooms on either side of the hall, with the doors open."

"Funny sort of woman, isn't she?" Tabby whispered as we left the kitchen. "All alone here and prone to attacks. What if she'd really hurt herself? If we hadn't been here she might be eaten by wild cats."

"Yes, because I saw a whole pack of them on the stairs, watching us, ready to strike." Hugh shook his head and smiled. "The house of the flying cats. Whatever will you come up with next, Tabby?"

We went to the car to get our bags, and that's when we saw a shiny black convertible pulling up the long driveway. A tall, slim man got out, wearing an overcoat and a long scarf. I guessed he was about twenty years old. He wore black leather boots and had bright blue eyes, and you could tell he hadn't shaved for a few days.

"This can't be the neighbour's boy," Tabby whispered.

"I'm here to see about the park keeper's job. My name's Duncan." He reached out and shook our hands. "Is Rose about? She said I should come in and have a chat with her."

"A park keeper driving a car like this? Makes you wonder what he does the rest of the time." I could see the wheels turning in Tabby's head.

# The Burial Chamber

"Pleased to meet you. I'm Hugh, and this is Tabitha and Mabel. Rose feels a bit unwell. Could I ask you to come back another time?"

Stepping aside, I could see long rods with pie-shaped disks at the end sticking out of the back of Duncan's car. They looked like metal detectors. Before we knew it, Rose was standing behind us at the front door, looking better.

"You must be Duncan. Please come in and have some tea."

"Don't mind if I do. Nice to meet ye all. Are ye related to Rose?"

"We're here on our summer holiday," Tabby said. "We're not relations, though. Mabel's mum heard about Rose and how she wanted to have some students to stay, so here we are."

"Very good." Duncan shut the front door of his car. "I expect to be seeing ye again." Then he winked at Tabby.

"Did you see him wink at me? I bet I've gone red all over."

"You look fine. I'm sure he was just being friendly." Hugh opened the car door and lifted our bags out for us. I remembered the first day we'd met at school and he'd carried my bag up the front steps and inside. I would never have dreamed that the very next summer we'd be together in Scotland.

Once inside, we started up the staircase. I counted thirty steps. "Her sister wrote some books. They're on the table at the bottom of the staircase. We should take a look at them."

"Any crunched-up skeletons inside them?" Hugh asked.

"The skeleton girl I saw hasn't aged well."

# The Burial Chamber

"That might be because she spent a few thousand years lying in a muddy bed, I'll bet." Hugh made a face at Tabby. "That's what you'll look like if you're not careful and you leave all that mud on your face."

"It's a skin cleanser, but if I leave it on too long I do get a rash."

Hugh looked at me and I couldn't help laughing.

On the second floor we walked along a mint-green carpeted floor past walls covered in light floral wallpaper with a yellow background.

"Two open doors." Tabby pushed ours back. "I bet you're in there, Hugh, because this side faces the water." We saw floral fabric everywhere. Both beds had canopies with green curtains.

Tabby jumped up on her bed. "Finally, I've realized my dream of being on stage." She pulled up the fabric curtain and hid behind it; then she peeked out showing only her face. "Thank you to my family and to my best friend, Mabel, for always believing in me." She made the sound of music playing her off and collapsed on the bed, giggling.

"I'm glad it's you sharing the room with Tabby. You'll be up half the night." Hugh left and went across the hall.

"One day, your name will be in lights, Tabby. I'm going to see Hugh's room."

"Don't be *long*." Tabby chided me.

I walked across the hall.

"Hugh?"

"Out here. There's a balcony."

I passed the double bed and a room decorated like ours. Hugh looked out at the drive.

"He's still there."

# The Burial Chamber

"There's bound to be lots to talk about keeping up an estate like this. Maybe we should get a head start on him."

"You're not even here five minutes, Mabel, and here you are off searching for another adventure."

We heard the chime of a bell coming from a board beside his bathroom door.

"Calling all love birds, Mabel, Hugh, are you in there? Should you really be alone? I may have to ring your parents."

"We're here." Hugh went in and pushed the button on the wall for Miss. Dundas's room. "Come and see my room, Tabby."

"I'll be right over."

"Bring your boots." I couldn't wait to get going.

Minutes later, we were at the foot of the stairs with our boots on. Just as we got outside, we saw someone riding a bicycle. He rode right up to us and stopped sharply, making a little skid.

"I'm Tom." He pulled down his orange anorak hood revealing a mop of red shaggy hair.

"Rose said you might be by." Hugh looked him up and down.

"I live over there." He pointed to a small farmhouse about a mile away. "Rose lets me come by quite often to help her. We don't have telly either, so I come around and watch with Rose until dinnertime. What do ye all do?" Tom rested his hands on the handlebars of his banana-seat bike.

"At the moment we're getting away from our parents for the summer, but it's only been one day so I might be in tears by tomorrow." Tabby looked at Tom and smiled.

# The Burial Chamber

"Would ye fancy a trip around the estate? The Knights Templar used to live here once. Ye know who they were, don't ye?" Tom asked.

"Everyone knows about those Christian soldiers from the Middle Ages. I'm Tabby, by the way." She reached out to shake his hand. "This is Mabel Hartley and Hugh McGinley. You might have heard of us on the news?"

"No, I don't believe I have but the pleasure's all mine." Tom shook Tabby's hand and held it for a few seconds. He got off his bike and put the kickstand down. "Let's start around the back."

We followed him along a path that ran beside the house. When we reached the back, we saw rose bushes in three large flowerbeds. To the left, beyond the roses, tennis courts looked back at us sadly.

"Do you play tennis?" Tabby asked. She was walking behind Tom and we brought up the rear.

"I can if I'm pressed to. Ye're probably a Wimbledon type though, aren't ye?"

"Maybe we could play sometime while we're here?" Tabby suggested.

"Don't let her fool you, Tom. She plays to win. You know the type." Hugh hated playing with Tabby because she always beat him.

"Not many of ye left, are there? I like a wee bit of spirit."

Tabby looked back at me and pointed at Tom. "He even likes tennis," she mouthed.

We walked on, seeing heavily-treed forest behind the tennis courts and the carving of a man in the top of a tree trunk. We came to a big muddy field about as long as a football pitch. It had a drop-

# The Burial Chamber

off on the edge and a sunken pit. Someone had been cutting blocks of earth out of it.

"This must be the peat bog." Tabby liked researching everything. At school, she worked as a tour guide on the grounds during the holidays. "Usually it's used for heat, like coal. Rose must sell it in the summer, so it's dried out for wintertime."

"I help with the cutting, one of my many odd jobs. The bog stretches to over there." Tom pointed away to the left. "Ye can't see it from here, but there's way more of it back there."

"And what's going on over there by the road?" Hugh pointed across the field.

A group of people were standing in an area on the very edge of the field.

"They're treasure hunters. Mind you, I've not seen that brown van before. They must have a new one with them."

"From here it looks as if they've got walking sticks." Tabby squinted, trying to make them out.

"They're metal detectors, just like in the back of Duncan's car." I jumped into the shallow pit and crouched down in front of the dark mucky soil, hoping we might find something like a piece of gold.

"If we walk along a bit towards the forest, I can show you this place, it's hidden from everyone. You can't even see it from the house. Come and see the steps hidden in the trees."

Hugh helped me back up and we walked for several more minutes. Tom stopped just before we reached a ridge that led down into a field.

"See. Take a look at this." He crouched down and pulled back the grass. Underneath we saw blocks of stone about two feet long.

# The Burial Chamber

"How many of them are there?" Tabby asked.

"Only five or six."

Walking down the steps, we saw a field sheltered by low trees on the ridge above. The wind picked up in the treetops and I closed my eyes.

"Gertrude used to believe that people might have worshipped here." Tom stood beside me.

"What would they have worshipped?" I licked my fingertip and held it up to see which way the wind was blowing.

"The sun," Tabby piped up. "Many thousands of years ago."

"Rose said Gertrude died. What was she like, anyway?" I asked.

"She was a bit of a bore. Hard to like really. I feel bad saying that but she liked people better dead than alive. She never stopped going on about mummies in the mud."

"Will you stay, Tom, to show us around the house?" Tabby urged.

"Can't today. Got one of my odd jobs to do and you'd best get yourselves settled in." Tabby looked disappointed.

"I could take ye around tomorrow or the day after. The Loch Ness Centre's not so bad and Urquhart Castle's well worth seeing. Do any of ye know how to drive?" He took a cigarette out of his pocket and lit it. We all stared at him.

"I suppose ye don't smoke, either?"

## Chapter Three

"Everything all right, children?" Rose was sitting with Duncan, sipping her tea. "Oh, I see ye've met Tom. How are ye Tom?"

"Quite well, thanks, and pleased to meet your boarders here. I can't stay, though."

"Pity," Rose said.

"Good to meet ye all. I'll give ye a day or two to settle in, then we'll have a poke about, how's that?" Tom left and we watched him hop on his banana seat bike and ride away down the drive.

"He seems nice enough," Hugh said. "How about we explore the rest of the house ourselves? Would that be all right with you, Rose?"

"By all means."

We spent the next hour opening doors and peeking into rooms. The old library on the second storey had a huge fireplace and a wooden table down the centre. A silver chandelier hung above the table and Persian rugs covered the floor. Around the fireplace, various farm scenes of rural Scotland decorated the walls. At the far end, we saw a cabinet with some statues and more armchairs and a desk. As we walked down the length of the room, we passed an archway about ten feet high and some steps going down into an area with many more books.

"I could live in this room alone. Of course someone would have to bring me food and drink, but I'd never want to leave," Tabby said.

We left the library and passed a beamed dining room with a painted ceiling and then a room with a

# The Burial Chamber

staircase at the back. A large tapestry of a tree in a garden hung on the far wall and in front of it was a desk, with a shelf that had several books on it. On the desk there were letters addressed to Rose and all sorts of gardening magazines, diaries and ledgers open. Across from the desk stood a chaise lounge with brown upholstery.

"Let's go upstairs." Tabby saw the huge bedroom with the enormous canopy bed first. "I wouldn't sleep a wink in here. I wonder if the canopy's ever fallen down on anyone? It would be just my luck to have it come down on top of me."

"Your luck's not that bad, Tabby," I said.

"Not half as good as yours, Mabel." I had been lucky, especially since I'd taken an interest in finding long-lost things.

Half an hour later, we'd been up to the third floor turret where we peeked out to admire the surrounding views, and now we felt in desperate need of something to drink.

"Let's make one more run down this hall and then we'll have made the rounds." Hugh tried the handle of the last door on the right. It opened easily. Inside, everything looked dark, from the chairs, to the walls, to the ceiling.

"Not exactly a party room, is it?" Tabby went over to inspect the coat of arms above the fireplace. Round wooden portraits hung between mounted deer heads.

"Maybe their father hunted. All these deer heads make me feel a bit sick. Let's get out of here and find those drinks." We followed Tabby out of the room, glad to close the door behind us.

+++

28

# The Burial Chamber

Next morning I wanted to explore Inverness and Rose told us we could borrow the bikes she kept in the carriage house to the left of the house. The other carriage house was "off limits". I desperately wanted to know why, but she wouldn't say anymore. Instead, she made us a picnic lunch and asked us to be home for dinner because she planned to make roast lamb for us. I hoped she wouldn't bump her head again. We had the whole day and as we expected the ride to take an hour we packed our jumpers and socks in case the wind came up.

Rose gave us the key and sent us off with our knapsacks. The carriage house had been converted from a stable and we found it full of all sorts of garden tools and machinery. In the back corner were, at least five bikes that looked as if they ought to have been taken to the dump.

"Will we even get down the driveway on those?" Tabby wondered. "Looks to me as if they haven't seen the light of day for years. What's over here in the corner under all that plastic? Oh, I hate to think."

"Let's pull this back." Hugh crouched down and touched the edge of the plastic.

"Mabel, give me a hand, would you?"

"Now that's more like it! Motor scooters; in fact I think they're Vespas!" Hugh went over and sat on the red one after we'd pulled off all the plastic. "Who wants to go and ask Rose about these? I'll bet she'll let us. Mabel, would you ask her? She likes you best."

I went inside and found Rose in the kitchen, unsure what she'd say.

# The Burial Chamber

"Did ye find the bikes all right?"

"Yes, we found them, but we also found the Vespas."

"They're mine, ye know; I don't get out on them much anymore. Gertrude never liked the things." Rose rinsed the potatoes in the sink.

"You probably wouldn't want us to take them out, would you?"

"Ye're welcome to, just be very careful. I don't fancy having to make a call to your parents if ye're in an accident. The keys are in the basket there by the toaster. Go on, have a bit of fun."

I found the keys. "We'll be very careful, I promise you."

"I know ye will, Mabel Hartley. Ye're a good lassie. Off ye go and call if ye need any help."

When I got back outside, I held the keys up in the air. Hugh let out a whoop. Tabby didn't look so sure.

"Why don't we ride together? You can go on the back," I said to her.

"You know how to ride these?"

I nodded, thinking I'd get the hang of it. "I'm sure Hugh can give me a few pointers. Don't worry, I'll be careful. They don't go that fast anyway. We won't tip over, I promise."

Hugh strapped on his own helmet, then came over and helped me with mine. I liked it when he touched my face and lifted my chin to secure the straps. He showed me the accelerator and the brakes and gave me a few tips on managing turns and parking.

Tabby got on behind me. Once we had gone up the drive and out onto the road we kept passing

# The Burial Chamber

fields of shaggy grass and hedgerows. As we got closer to the city we saw more views of the sweeping valley. A steam train chugged along, billowing a great white cloud of smoke. We slowed down, merging with the traffic, and came up a narrow road, passing several tall houses with chimney pots on top of the roof.

I signalled and pulled over, remembering the map I'd brought from our room. Minutes later we parked the Vespas in front of a glass building, with the Scots flag on the top.

"What are we doing here, Mabel?" Tabby took off her helmet.

"Just a little research. It's the Tourist Information Centre."

As we opened the door, bagpipes started to play with a rolling drum.

"It's the door chime. Look at that." I opened the door again. "I've been waiting to hear bagpipes ever since we got here and I haven't seen any tartan yet either."

"The tartan shop's just down the street on the left." A thin man with a doughy face and huge bushy eyebrows came out from behind a curtain and stopped to face us at the counter, sucking the nib of a pipe. He wore a brown knitted waistcoat with pockets and buttons down the front.

"Not often I see such young people in here. My name's Mr. Spotswood, and where would you all be from?"

"We're from Hampshire." I stepped forward. "I'm Mabel Hartley. This is Tabitha Mason and Hugh McGinley. We're here on holiday, staying just out of town at Rose Blythe's house. Do you know her?"

# The Burial Chamber

"We're old friends. I'd know those Vespas anywhere. We went to primary school together. You must have been the ones we saw up there behind her house. I wondered who was staying with her. I'm not sure how she manages with her sister gone. But that's why she's having lodgers, to keep her company."

"Were you looking for something in the field?" Hugh asked beside me.

"Och, we're always looking for something to turn in our hands, some relic of ages past. And who knows what might come out of that bog? So much has already."

"Where are those things now?" Tabby felt suspicious too.

"In the British Museum, but only some of them go there. We can't be too careful. They're not all like me; some treasure hunters will sell what they find without telling a soul, and others will keep the treasure for themselves. Most of it's from the Bronze Age, 3,000 to 5,000 years ago. The cape got them started."

"The cape?" I hadn't read about that yet.

"Aye, the one they found in Wales in the 1800s. And they say one could be found here too."

"Who would say that?" Hugh asked.

"Locals." Mr. Spotswood took a puff on his pipe. "We've found a number of the same kind of amber beads that were found with the Welsh Cape. Folks around here think there's a connection."

"You mean because the people may have been on a route trading beads?" Tabby knew all about it already.

"Full marks, lassie."

# The Burial Chamber

"Do you know anything more about the cape?" Hugh came in closer.

"They called it the Mold Gold Cape because they found it in an ancient burial mound in Mold, which is in Flintshire, in Wales. In 1833, some workers uncovered a stone-lined burial chamber, with the cape inside."

"What happened then?" I asked.

"They divided some of the pieces up amongst themselves, but then someone sold the largest piece to the British Museum. They say the cape is one of the most important European Bronze Age finds of objects that were worn for ceremonial purposes. I have a book from the British Museum right here. I can show you." He opened the book, and flipped through until he reached the part he was looking for.

*At the centre of the mound, the crushed gold cape lay with the fragmentary remains of a skeleton and strips of amber beads. One of the finest examples of prehistoric sheet-gold working, the cape came from a single ingot of gold.*

"What's an ingot?" Tabby asked.

"A block of gold or silver." He kept reading.

*Embellished with ribs and bosses, which mimic multiple strings of beads amid folds of cloth, the perforations indicate it had a lining, perhaps of leather.*

He handed me the book and showed me the photo. I'd expected something long and flowing, but the cape looked short, more like a collar, fitted across the shoulders. "How unusual. And they think someone wore this?" I showed Tabby and Hugh the picture too.

# The Burial Chamber

"Aye, it would have pinned their arms to their sides, but I imagine the honour of wearing it would have outweighed the discomfort."

"Have you found anything yourself up at the peat bog behind the house?" Hugh looked up from the picture.

From his pocket, Mr. Spotswood took something. He stretched out his other hand and put it in the middle of his palm. We all looked at a dark, brown bead. It had a small hole through the middle for a string. When I reached over, Mr. Spotswood said, "Aye, aye, aye! I can't be letting ye touch the amber bead, love. It's too good. But Inverness still has lots to give, I'm sure."

"Why do you keep that in your pocket?" I asked. "Shouldn't it be in a museum?"

He looked at me steadily for a few seconds. "They'll not miss just one bead. I keep it as a reminder of what we might find with a bit of luck. Ye can understand that, can't ye, Mabel?"

I didn't like the way he said my name or how he smiled when he closed his hand and tucked the bead back into his waistcoat pocket.

"We have about fifty Clava cairns around Inverness. I've even found some myself. People say I've a nose for the cairns."

"What are they like?" Tabby asked.

"Oh, circular chamber tombs, with the entrance oriented southwest towards the mid-winter sunset. Some have stone paths forming rays away from the central burial chamber. Ye might go and look at a few that are out there by the old Culloden battlefield. Rose would know where they are to be found. She could take ye. I found the first one when I was but ten years old."

Mr. Spotswood shut the book. "I've read all Gertrude's books. 'Tis a pity she's no longer with us. I never knew her well. With her gone, Rose really needs someone to help her manage the estate. She thinks she can do it all by herself, but with her asthma, she has to come to her senses soon."

"Someone called Duncan came to see her about a park keeper job," Tabby said.

"Did he now?" Mr. Spotswood mulled it over.

"Do you know him?" Hugh asked.

"Aye, he's been out with us a few times. Archaeology's his game. I believe he's studying for his third degree, a Ph.D., I think."

"Why would he want a park keeper job at Roses's? I knew we sounded nosy but I didn't care.

"I expect he wants a bit more money, and getting a bit closer to that part of the bog wouldn't hurt either." Mr. Spotswood sucked the end of his pipe.

"Thank you for your time; you've been awfully helpful." I felt like a bit of fresh air.

"Do come back if ye need anything. Take my card, in fact, and let me know if ye find anything worth seeing. I'd be interested." I took it knowing he'd be the last person I'd call about anything.

## Author biography

Jane Reddington is a Canadian author who lives on Gabriola Island in British Columbia, Canada with her husband and two children.

She loves everything that Mabel Hartley lets her do – travel to far off places, learn about history and go on adventures. Most of all she loves writing books and sharing them with readers.

Visit www.janereddington.com to find out more about Mabel Hartley and her adventures.

Made in the USA
Columbia, SC
28 August 2018